I0687792

THE RISE

DROWNED EARTH

DROWNED EARTH

Eight novellas.
Eight Australian authors.
One watery apocalypse.

Scientists said that it would take 5000 years for Earth's
oceans to rise.

They were wrong.

After an asteroid collides with Antarctica, a tsunami
devastates the world's coastal cities and escalates the melting
of the ice caps.

These eight novellas set in various locations around Australia
explore the potential consequences of such a catastrophe.
They can be read in any order.

Prequel short story: Shards of Silver by Alanah Andrews
Submerged City by Austin P. Sheehan
The Rise by Sue-Ellen Pashley
Fire Over Troubled Water by Nick Marone
Tides of War by Marcus Turner
The Jindabyne Secret by Jo Hart
River of Diamonds by S. M. Isaac
Salvaged by C.A. Clark
Emoto's Promise by Shel Calopa

THE RISE

SUE-ELLEN PASHLEY

DROWNED EARTH

First published by Deadset Press in 2019

www.aussiespeculativefiction.com

Copyright ©2019 Sue-Ellen Pashley

Sue-Ellen Pashley has asserted their right to be identified as the author of their work in accordance with the Copyright, Designs and Patents Act 1988

ISBN: 978-0-6484211-4-6

All rights reserved. No part of this publication may be reproduced, stored in a retrieval system, or transmitted, in any form or by any means, electronic, mechanical, photocopying, recording or otherwise, without the prior permission of the publishers

Cover design Copyright © Alanah Andrews

Edited by Alanah Andrews & Austin P. Sheehan

www.aussiespeculativefiction.com

DEDICATION

To Adrian, for everything, for always.

CHAPTER ONE

The body in the water bumps almost lovingly against the side of my boat, kissing it gently before the movement of the ocean separates them again. I take an involuntary step back, the shock of seeing someone face down, half lying on a piece of wood in the pre-dawn light overwhelming. Which is crazy. This isn't my first body—far from it. I'm the medic for our Territory, for God's sake. But it's been five years since the Great Rise and a long time since bodies have washed up on the small amount of land the ocean has left us to exist on.

The shock only lasts a moment before my training kicks in. I grab the gaff hook from the side of the boat and reach out, trying to get a hold of the clothes without damaging the flesh. The wood makes the body bob as I try to snag it, moving it further away, and it takes two more attempts before I'm able to hook the jacket. I walk carefully to the landing platform at the back of the boat, bringing the body with me like a dog on a leash.

Bending down, I grab the jacket and haul the person onto the landing, turning them face up. The shock of seeing his face paralyses me for a second—everything except my heart, which is pounding in my chest as if it's trying to make up for the stillness. And then my hand is reaching out to touch the wound on his cheek, on his forehead, touching and then pulling away like a bird uncertain of where to land.

"No. No, no, no. Mason." Louder. "Mason!" But there's no response. I lean forward, bringing my cheek to his mouth. He's not breathing!

God, oh God.

Checking that there's nothing blocking his airways, I pull him further onto the deck, grunting and huffing, wishing, not for the first time, that I was taller than five foot two, and start CPR.

"Come on, come on," I mutter, pushing the heels of my palms into his chest.

And then he's coughing, water gushing out of his mouth, his nose, and I roll him on his side. Sitting on my heels for a second, I watch him breathe and let out my own breath, trying to get my thoughts together. I don't know how to make sense of what's happening—whether there's been a terrible accident or . . . something else. I take another deep breath, needing to concentrate, needing to make sure he's okay.

It's only when I take off his jacket that I see the blood soaking his light blue shirt. I lift the material. The wound's still bleeding and I wipe it with the edge of his jacket before applying pressure. It looks like a stab wound. Which doesn't make sense.

Who the hell would want to stab Mason? Christ!

My head whips around, as if I can feel eyes on me, watching us, plotting. And yet, that's crazy. Crazy! Violence isn't tolerated. Not since the Territories were divided. Not since the uprising almost three years ago. Any sort of violence is dealt with by banishment—a passive violence really. Because being sent out onto the endless ocean is basically a death sentence.

Maybe it was an accident then. Maybe he slipped and fell onto something. Yet the incision is clean, like a weapon's been shoved in and pulled out, rather than tearing at the skin. Or am I just imagining things?

None of that matters now though. I need to stop the bleeding. I run into the cabin and grab my medic bag before kneeling beside him again. The wound is going to need cleaning and stitches, and something to avoid possible infection. At least I have enough turmeric powder with me—I'm grateful I took the time to make some last week when I noticed supplies were getting low. The Authority's only given me so much growing room for medicinal plants on the land, so I've taken to growing things on the boat as well, and turmeric is worth its weight in gold.

I clean the wound, sprinkling the powder on, before getting the needle ready, my shaking hands making threading difficult. I can only hope there's no serious internal damage. I don't think there will be, given the placement of the wound. There's nothing I can do anyway. Not really. Not without access to a proper operating theatre. And I only have a few of the operating instruments I used in my first two years of medical school. I just have to hope it won't be an issue—pray to whatever God still exists in our new world—and try to stop the blood loss.

By the time I turn back, the turmeric's done its job, stopping most of the bleeding. Mason's stomach muscles contract and I hear the hiss of breath as the needle pierces his skin, which I take as a good sign. It only takes a few minutes to stitch the wound, and I wind a bandage around his stomach as the sun crests the horizon. Soon, everyone else will be up too. They'll see Mason and have questions—questions that can't be answered. Not by me, anyway.

Gripping him under his arms, I drag him towards the door of the cabin. Because even though it'd probably be the right thing—the smart thing—to alert the Authority and let them sort it out, whatever 'it' is, Mason is my friend. My best friend. I need to protect him for a while, until I know what's happened. I'm grateful, for once, that I couldn't sleep and was the one to find him floating in the water.

We're through the doorway when he murmurs and I lie him on the deck, touching his face again. "Mason? It's okay. You're safe."

He blinks, confusion evident in his eyes, before he focuses on me. "Katie. Katie girl."

I smile at his name for me, wanting to cry and rage and laugh, all at the same time. A ball of conflicting emotions ricochets through my body, my mind, not giving me a chance to grab hold of it. "You're okay," I say again, wondering if I'm trying to convince Mason or myself.

His hand comes up to grip my wrist, strong even with the loss of blood. "Don't let them find me, Katie. Promise." His voice his hoarse, his face pale.

"Who?"

He blinks, staring up at me with those earnest eyes I know so well. I lean in so I can hear him. "The

Authority," he says before he passes out again.

I stare down at the unconscious body of my best friend, lying on the floor of my boat.

Shit!

CHAPTER TWO

It's almost impossible to get Mason up onto the bunk, and after the second attempt—where I accidentally hit his head on the side of the wood—I give it up as a bad joke. Pulling the quilt and pillow down from my bed instead, I set up a place on the floor, trying to make sure he's as comfortable as possible.

My thoughts are out of control, not giving me anything solid to focus on. I take a deep breath. And another one. I can do this. It doesn't matter that it's Mason laying there. Mason who taught me to fish, who held my hair back when I got drunk as a teenager, who knows me better than anyone alive. I can treat him as any other patient . . .

Because I know what I need to do—one step after another. This is what I've trained for. Easy. I bend down and listen to his breathing again. It's steadier, even though he hasn't regained consciousness.

Tick.

I check the wound, making sure our journey inside hasn't torn any stitches.

Tick.

Then put him into the recovery position.

Tick.

But now I've made him comfortable, my control wavers. I stare down at him, trying to make another decision, my heart a jittery mess as I watch him.

This is Mason. Mason!

Who I nearly lost this morning . . .

If I'd been looking the other way, if the current hadn't made him bump against my boat . . . my heart squeezes, so painfully I actually press my hand against my chest, trying to ease it.

Christ. None of this makes sense. It feels like three years ago, when everything shitty was happening. Five years ago even, after the Rise. I grip my fingers together, tight, letting the slight pain keep me focused, keep me grounded.

Breathe.

I step out of the room, looking over the water as

the sun paints it gold. I can't stay here, as much as I want to. Someone will come looking for me, wondering what's keeping me from working for our Territory. Worried about me. As their medic, I'm important to the group. And some of them are good friends. But allowing anyone to come onto the boat is out of the question. I stand straighter and step out onto the deck.

Steven, my neighbour to the left, is already rowing towards shore, his movements strong and sure— five years of practice evident.

"Morning, Kate." His voice carries easily across the water and I give him a small wave in response. "Want me to come and get you?"

"No, you're good." I'm pleased to hear my voice sounds normal, even if my brain is still playing catch up. "I've got to come back in a few hours and check on . . . a herbal mix I've got going."

He laughs. "Well, can't say I like the smell of most of your mixes, but I'm glad you keep making them."

I smile back. Some of the herbals I make *are* pungent but, given that any sort of pharmaceutical is hard to come by, I've needed to adapt. Our whole world has needed to adapt. Well, the ones of us left anyway. The fact I was only two years into my medical training before the Rise probably made it easier for me. Dr Sabor— who'd been in his late seventies when it happened—

struggled for the last four years of his life, no longer having access to the tools he'd always been able to call on.

I untie my dinghy from the boat and climb in. It's crazy to think I'd only been on a boat twice in my life before the Rise. But then, there isn't a person alive who hasn't had their life radically changed by the asteroid's collision with Earth. Jagannatha—the piece of space rock that changed our world forever.

Rowing over, I tie my dinghy to the rails placed on the edge of our Territory—Territory One. One of nine. Not particularly inventive names but the numbers do the job. It's our home now, no matter what it's called. I step onto the rough-hewn stairs, built to stop further erosion from all of us coming and going each day. The super storms we have to put up with in our new world do enough damage.

"Morning, Kate."

I look up to see a young girl—almost a woman, I have to keep reminding myself—perched on top of a rock jutting out over the water, grinning down at me. Ellie was only eleven when the Great Rise took everyone she'd ever known. At least Mason and I'd had each other—best friends since five, when he shared his lamington with me at preschool.

Ellie had been alone for three months, marooned

in her house on a small piece of land that'd become an island. I can't imagine how terrifying that must've been. It was only thanks to Carl, the leader of the Authority and the person who'd set up the Territories, giving us all somewhere to live, that she'd been saved. I'd helped to nurse her back to health and she'd adopted me as a big sister, deciding that she wanted to train as a medic. It's been nice, and mentoring Ellie's given me something to focus on other than a life which no longer existed.

"You're late this morning."

I smile back at her, feeling slightly more at ease for the first time since finding Mason. "Or maybe you're early."

She slides down the side of the rock to meet me on the path. "Are we picking herbs this morning?"

I nod. "Where's your kayak?"

After living with me for so long, last year Ellie had decided she needed her own space. Fifteen felt too young, but you don't survive what we'd all gone through—her especially—without growing up faster than kids used to. Mason had found her a small sailboat which they'd fixed up for her to live on and a kayak rather than a dinghy to get around on. I'd laughed when she'd said dinghies were for old people.

She nods towards the shed where we store the food. "I dragged it up behind. Hey, do you know when

Mason will be back? My paddle's got a crack. It's not too bad at the moment but he was going to try and find me another one."

I swallow hard, trying to keep my face calm at the mention of his name. God, I'm being paranoid. This is Ellie, for Christ's sake. And yet, Mason's been stabbed. Stabbed! Left for dead. And I definitely don't need her involved in something that even I don't understand yet.

"No, he didn't say." And then I think of something I should have thought about earlier. "You haven't seen his boat?"

She shakes her head as she walks in front of me up the path. Another mystery, then. One that makes his avoidance of the Authority—our 'government'—even more disturbing. Our Territory is a small community, a family on steroids, which makes it hard to believe he could've been stabbed without an uproar. Someone must have seen something. Heard something. That this could have happened without anyone noticing is almost beyond belief.

"Everything okay?" Ellie stops on the trail between the rows of carrots and beans, turning back to look at me.

I nod, catching up with her. "Yeah, sorry. Million miles away. Just thinking about what herbs we need today."

She watches me for a moment, as if she's trying to work out what I'm not saying—too observant for her own good.

I smile and start up the trail again, forcing her to continue on. "Come on, slowpoke. We've got herbs to pick and poultices to make."

It's enough, evidently, to satisfy her that things are okay because she chats normally as we climb the terraced land. I let her words wash over me, my mind going back to Mason, unconscious in the water, floating away . . .

"Are you even listening to me?" Ellie's hands on her hips tell me she already knows the answer to that.

"Yes." She raises an eyebrow and I smile. "Actually, no. Sorry."

Mason's always teasing me about the fact I'm a terrible liar. Shit, everything seems to come back to him this morning . . .

Ellie points out over our Territory. "I said the potatoes must be ready for harvesting. God. Roast potatoes are the best."

I laugh at the longing in her voice and look to where she's pointing, watching Steven and several of the others work their way across the terrace.

We've got one of the steepest Territories out of the nine that make up our region, right on the edge of the

Sunshine Coast Hinterland, making it harder to farm and more dangerous in the superstorms. But, since we're right on the water, it means we don't have to use any of our precious land to live on, so most of us feel it's worth it. The terracing had been a nightmare though, and I still shiver at the back-breaking work we'd had to do without machinery . . . and the number of injuries that had occurred.

Looking out over Territory One, I can see the rest of our community—either already on land or just arriving in their boats. There isn't any space for someone who doesn't work. Even Beryl, at eighty-seven, spends her days washing the vegetables, ready for consumption or bartering.

My herbs are up on the steepest part of the land—the area least useful to any other crop. Not that anyone's ever said that. They've all, at some stage, been helped by the mixtures I've made. Five years of going up and down the side of the mountain . . . I'd probably be able to do it with my eyes shut. Not that I'd ever try. One miss-step and I'd be tumbling headlong into the nearby valley.

I come up beside Ellie and stroke my hands over the leaves of the plants—chamomile, echinacea, lavender, mint, thyme, comfrey, rosemary, yarrow—and the smell rises up, greeting me.

"So, what do we need today?" Ellie asks.

I run off a list of herbs for her and she moves around confidently, picking what we need while I weed the beds, keeping them clear for the plants to grow. Most days, I love this part of the job, even though I wasn't much of a gardener before the Rise. It's usually calming. All I can think about now though, is Mason—wondering if he's still unconscious, wondering what happened to him . . .

"Kate. Hey, Kate."

At the bottom of the terraces, Gavin is waving at me as he calls out. My stomach lurches, like it's taken a tumble down the hill to meet him. Gavin Anderson, our leader for the three years we've been a Territory and our representative on the Authority. And he's obviously wanting me to come down.

Shit.

Is he involved in whatever's happened to Mason? Does he know I've got him on my boat?

Ellie's watching me, obviously noting my hesitation. She frowns but I speak before she can. "You okay to do the rest on your own?"

She nods, eyes narrowed, but at least she doesn't question me. I make my way down the terraces before curiosity can get the better of her.

Gavin watches me, hands on his hips, a frown on

his face. I try not to jump to conclusions—our representative on the Authority isn't a smiler and hasn't been in the five years I've known him. Still, Mason's warning swirls in my brain, making me feel slightly nauseous.

Gavin nods in greeting as I stop in front of him. "Territory Three's asked for a medic."

It's something I usually appreciate about him—his lack of small talk, always straight to the point. But this morning, I want talk. Information. Anything that'll help me make sense of finding my friend floating on the waves with a hole in his side.

"Why do they need me?"

His frown increases, the lines in his forehead looking permanently embedded. "I don't know. They just asked for you. Is it going to be a problem?"

I shake my head, heart thumping uncomfortably in my chest. It's not an unusual request—there aren't many medics to go around the different Territories and I often have to help one of the others. "No. I'm happy to go. Just wondering what I'll need to take."

He looks at me for a few seconds before shrugging. Those seconds don't do my heart any favours. "They didn't say." Gavin gestures behind me. "Can Ellie finish for you up there?"

"Yes. She knows what she's doing." I take a deep

breath, watching Gavin's face as I ask my next question. "Any idea when Mason's due back?"

His eyes move to focus somewhere behind my shoulder. I struggle not to look around, waiting to see if he'll look back at me.

"Nope. He'll be back when he's back, I guess."

And still he doesn't meet my eyes. It's not unusual for Gavin, but this morning, I don't know if it means more… means something else, and I feel my heartrate quicken. I always liked—and trusted—him, but now . . .

He bends down to pluck a weed out of one of the gardens. "Why?"

I shrug. "No big reason. He was going to help Ellie fix her paddle." It sounds lame, even to my ears but it's the only thing I can come up with. Mason's right. I am a crap liar.

Gavin stands up, dusting the soil from his hands. "Well, I can't tell you anything. Mason's never worked to a timetable."

Which is true. But it doesn't help me to know if I can trust Gavin or not. He's always been a bit socially awkward, so it's hard to tell if he's being his normal awkward self, or if he's played a part in hurting Mason. Does he think Mason's dead body has being swept out to sea, never to be seen again? But why would he—would anybody—want to hurt Mason?

"Okay," I say carefully, "well, if you hear he's back, can you let me know?"

"Sure. Although he usually comes to see you first anyway, doesn't he?"

There's something to his question, something I can't quite put a finger on. "Most times, I guess."

He holds my gaze for a moment and then nods once before turning and walking further along the terraces. "Just make sure you get over to Three today," he calls over his shoulder. "They need you."

I sigh, wondering what they need me for. At least it gives me an excuse to go back to the boat for supplies before heading over. I start walking down to the water, careful to step on the worn groove of the path. I don't need to turn to know the pounding footsteps behind me are Ellie's.

"Hey, can I come too?"

I glance over my shoulder. "How do you know I'm going anywhere?"

She snorts. "I'm not stupid. You're heading back to your boat. It must be to get supplies. Where are you going?"

"Over to Three. They've asked for a medic."

She catches up with me, walking behind me on the narrow path. "That'll be one of the Morganson boys. I heard he fell off a rock last night."

I look back and then shake my head. "How do you hear all of this? We're supposed to stick to our Territories."

I can hear the grin in her voice. "It's amazing what you hear when you take a leisurely paddle to relax at the end of the day."

I stop and turn around so I'm facing her. "I know you're not going to listen but be careful, okay?" Our Territories have been safe for the last three years. But now . . .

She frowns, a small line creasing the area between her eyebrows. "Why? What's happened?"

I feel the heat come to my cheeks. "What are you talking about? Nothing. Just be careful. People get suspicious about others being in their Territory."

She grins. "Not me. Everyone loves me."

I shake my head but have nothing to say to that. She's right.

"So? Can I come?"

"No. Not this time. I need you to get the herbs for me."

She holds out the bag. "Done."

Damn. I don't want her coming to the boat. She doesn't need to be involved in any of this. I take the bag from her, rougher than I should be. "No. I need to go on my own."

She cocks her head at me. "Why?"

My brain stutters, refusing to lock onto a valid reason. Why can I never think of a stupid lie when I need to? "Because." Not a great comeback really. It reminds me of something my mum would say when we were kids and my chest tightens at the thought of her, even after five years.

Ellie sighs. "What's going on?"

"Why do you keep asking that? Nothing! Nothing's going on!"

"Kate, you're like my big sister. That's why I can tell you honestly—you're a terrible liar."

I scowl at her. "Nothing is going on."

She snorts. I choose to ignore it and keep walking down the path, but it doesn't shut her up. "You know I'm going to follow you over on my kayak, don't you? Anyone else, I'd just do it without telling them, but you're my friend, so I'm giving you fair warning."

I chew the inside of my cheek, staring at the ground as we walk, trying to think. God, I can't let her get involved with this. I need to protect her. She's too young—way too young—just a kid . . . "Don't, Ellie. Please. Just . . . stay here. Let me handle this, okay?" My voice is soft, pleading.

"Handle what? You've never stopped me coming to one of the other Territories with you before."

I growl at her. Not effective, and not particularly mature, but I can't help it. "Ellie, stop. It's nothing you need to worry about."

She moves in front of me, hands on her hips, stopping me in my tracks. I can see Trish and George, two others in the Territory I count as friends, watching us from further along the terrace and my heart feels like it's dropped into my stomach acid. God, I don't need anyone focusing on me, wondering what's happening. Or maybe I'm being paranoid. There are good people in our Territory. People I can trust—or I'm fairly sure I can.

"I'm not a kid, Kate."

"You are."

"I'm not." Her lips are tight as she glares at me. "I was a kid, five years ago when the Rise happened. When I lost everyone. But I haven't been a kid since then. Since before Carl found me, when I was desperate, on my own. Not in all the times since then when we found bodies washed up every day on the shore, or in the super storms when we wondered if we'd survive, not in the fighting before the Territories were formed. I'm not a kid."

I know she's right. All of it's true. But that makes it even sadder. I want her to be able to be a kid. I want to protect her. "Ellie . . ."

"Kate. Just tell me what's happening."

I sigh. It's a sad sigh—a giving-in sigh. "I'll tell you on the way over to the boat."

She has the grace not to smile at her win, just nods and walks next to me in silence, taking the bag of herbs and roots from me and carrying them. She sits in the dinghy and grabs the oars while I untie it. I'm happy to let her row. Payback, maybe.

I chew the side of my lip, trying to find the right words. Not that there *are* any right words really.

"Mason's been hurt." There, the words are out.

She frowns at me. "What do you mean?"

"I was out on the deck this morning and found him face down, unconscious, in the water. He'd been stabbed."

"Stabbed? By who?"

I wave my hand and make a shushing noise at her. There isn't anyone close enough to hear but it's better to be safe than sorry. And sound carries well over water. "I don't know. But he woke up for a minute and told me not to tell anyone on the Authority."

"Shit! Do you think he did something wrong? That he's hiding from them so he doesn't get banished?"

I shake my head and stifle a sigh. It feels like I've been sighing all morning. "I don't know. I don't know what any of it means."

We're at the yacht and I tie the dinghy to the back

before climbing onto the deck, taking the bag from Ellie as she comes aboard.

"He's in my cabin," I say, and she follows me through.

Mason's still out to it on the floor—to be expected, I guess, given it's been less than an hour since I left. I feel more settled this time as I check on him. I wonder if it's because I have Ellie here with me as backup. Or maybe it's because I have someone to hold it together for. Mason's breathing is stronger, and the wound hasn't been bleeding so I roll him a little, trying to relieve any pressure points.

I touch his face, my fingers gentle. "Mason?"

There's no response and I turn to face Ellie, standing in the doorway. She looks white.

"You okay?"

She nods and then shakes her head before shrugging. "He looks . . . less. Like he's not really Mason. I've never seen him so . . . still."

I take her arm and turn her around. It's hard, seeing someone you're close to looking this way. Easier when it's a stranger. "I know it's hard but you need to keep it together, okay? Until he wakes up and can tell us why he doesn't want any of the Authority to know, we need to pretend we haven't seen him. That he's still out scavenging and fishing. Can you do that?"

She nods. This time it's stronger. Determined.

I gather my medic bag and check the stock in it before going back out on the deck. Ellie has already untied the dinghy and she's waiting for me, her face a picture of calm as if she hasn't just experienced the shock of seeing her friend badly injured. She's good at this. Much better than me.

We don't say anything on the way back over to Territory One. I don't really know what to say and Ellie looks lost in thought. Gavin's waiting for us, hands on hips, as we tie the dinghy to the rails again.

"You going over now?"

I hold up the bag for him to see. "Ellie's coming with me. We finished gathering the herbs we need."

He looks at Ellie and then nods. "They said they'd give some eggs in payment. Don't forget them when you come back. A dozen. Count them before you leave."

I hold back a sigh. No one's ever tried to short change me before and yet, Gavin gives me this lecture every time I go to help another Territory. It's like his head is still in the time when the Territories were fighting the rest of the survivors on the hinterland for every scrap of space, every resource . . . everything really.

"I know. I'll be back soon."

He watches us as we walk up the path that leads

to the other Territories, spread out across the mountains. I push against Ellie with my shoulder. "You okay?"

"Do you think he knows anything? About Mason being hurt?"

"I don't know. We'll just have to wait until Mason regains consciousness."

Which I hope will be by the time we get back, although I don't say that out loud. It's stupid but I don't want to jinx it by uttering the words. We skirt the edge of Territory Two, the only other Territory which borders the ocean, waving to the few who call out to us. Others stand and stare, watching every step we take. Things have definitely been better in the last three years but they still aren't great. There's still a lot of people who find it hard to trust . . . and hard to share. I guess Gavin isn't the only one stuck in the old ways.

Territory Three is further up the mountain and the small cabins they've built to house everyone sit along the edge of their land, squeezed so close together you can barely move between them. Every time I come to a landlocked Territory, I'm thankful for my little boat that isn't right on top of my neighbours, even if it's scary sometimes in the storms.

Alex, the Authority rep for Three, saunters over to us and smiles. He's a tall man, towering over us, but that isn't the thing that always puts me on guard around him. It's hard to say what it is exactly, except his smile never seems to reach his eyes. He's only ever been polite to me, but I can't help feeling that's due to the fact that it's usually one of his boys that brings me here.

"Morning ladies. Thanks for coming over on short notice."

I incline my head and lift the corners of my lips. "No worries. Who's the patient?"

He sighs, like his life is one big ball of difficult. "Jacob. Who else? He fell off a rock last night and hurt his wrist. We thought it might just be sprained but it's pretty swollen and sore this morning."

I nod. "Is he at your hut or in the communal area?"

"Our hut. Jen didn't want him running around, although trying to keep that kid still is as difficult as trying to lasso the moon."

Ellie laughs and he smiles at her, like he appreciates having a receptive audience. I guess that's why everyone loves her.

"Come on," says Alex, "I'll take you down there."

"We know the way if there's things you have to do."

He laughs, as if I'm making a joke. "I bet you do. No, no, all good. I'll take you. It's the least I can do."

I bite back a sigh. On the surface, he seems a nice

person. And, objectively, he's good looking—tall, broad shoulders, and a face that wouldn't have been out of place on TV before the Rise. But there's something about him that rubs me the wrong way. Gut feeling, as my gran used to say.

We follow him down the hill, past four huts before we come to theirs. Jacob is sitting on the small veranda and jumps up as we get close.

"Kate!" He grins at me and this time, it isn't hard to smile back. He's a cute kid—full of life, which is probably why I've seen him so often even though he's only eight.

"Hey, Jacob, I hear you've been in the wars."

He holds up his bandaged arm. "Yep. Fell off a rock. I was the first one up it though." His voice is filled with pride.

Alex puts a hand on his son's shoulder. "Where's your mum?"

"She went to get the eggs for Kate. Told me to wait out here so I don't mess up the house while she's gone."

Probably a good plan on Jen's part. I don't know how she does it. She and Alex already had four boys— including twins—before the Rise, and in the last five years, they've had another two. All six of them are whirlwinds.

"Guess it's just us then." Alex waves me towards a chair and stands behind Jacob, hands on his shoulders like he's trying to keep him in place in the other chair. Sitting, I unwind the bandage and look at his arm. The wrap's kept the swelling down a bit, but it's turned a good shade of black overnight. I feel carefully along the bone, noting Jacob's wince and the hiss of breath. His face has gone pale, so I know he's in pain, even if he's trying not to show it.

"Well, kiddo, I think you've broken it all right. But don't worry, I'm going to cast it for you." I look up at Alex. "I need some water for the plaster."

He nods but his hands clench into Jacob's shoulders and I see the young boy wince again. "That's going to have to come out of the family supply, Jake. I hope you know that."

"Yes, Dad. Sorry, Dad."

Alex taps his son on the shoulder, harder than seems necessary, and goes to the barrel that holds the family water. It's supposed to last them a week because even though we get the storms, collecting the water's another thing altogether when the water comes in horizontal. And in between the storms, there are a lot of sunny days that dry everything out. The world obviously still has some serious healing to do and, honestly, some days we're just holding on for the ride.

Alex brings the water over and passes it to me, his fingers touching mine as he does. I struggle not to withdraw my hand. He's not doing anything inappropriate—not at all—but still . . . I can't help my reaction. Every time. He smiles, like he knows—knows and thinks it's funny—and sits on the steps of the veranda. Watching us. I try not to let it bother me.

Grabbing two of the splint sticks from my kit, I get Ellie to hold them in place while I wrap Jake's arm in the bandage again, before I soak the strips of another bandage in a plaster mix Ellie's made, layering them around. It isn't as thick or as effective as before the Rise but then, a lot of things aren't as good. It's just a part of our lives now. Part of our adaptation.

Both the bandages and the plaster I have in stock are getting low but there's no point in keeping what we have. If they're needed now, they may as well be used. Hopefully we'll be able to get more, although—similar to all of the resources that existed before the Rise—most of them are lost to us. And the remaining resources are always jealously guarded.

Jacob fidgets as I layer the plaster and Ellie grabs his arm. "You need to keep still, otherwise Kate wouldn't be able to fix it properly."

He slumps his shoulders, as if we're asking the world. "Can I go climbing after this?"

"Not for a while. Stay off the rocks, okay?" I try to put on a stern face but he grins at me and I can't help grinning back.

"You'll be helping your mother with the chickens until your arm's better," Alex says, and Jacob groans.

"Chickens are boring!"

"What work do you want to do when you're bigger?" Ellie asks, and I'm grateful she's distracting him enough for me to finish.

"I want to be a fisher searcher, like Mason."

My heart trips over itself at hearing his name so casually mentioned, when all I can picture is him, lying like death on the floor of the boat. Ellie glances at me and I ignore her.

Jacob bounces his leg. "Did he bring anything good back this time?"

"Who?"

"Mason."

I swallow hard, trying to get some moisture into my suddenly dry mouth. "He's not back yet."

"Yes, he is," Jacob says, picking at the edge of the plaster. "I saw his boat last night when I was up on the rock."

My heart pounds as Jake's words seem to sit there in the silence. From the corner of my eye, I see Ellie's face go pale.

"Jake." Alex's voice is filled with warning. He moves closer to me, close enough that I can feel the heat from his body, almost threatening, and the hairs on my arms prickle uncomfortably. This reaction to Jake's comment about Mason isn't normal, is it? Was Alex involved with the incident . . . or do I just think that because it's Alex?

"Don't pick at the plaster," he says at last, and I force myself to relax, wondering if I'm just being paranoid. "Is he done?"

"Yes." I take a step back, wiping my hands on the towel.

"Okay mate, go and find your mum and get the eggs for Kate."

"Ellie, do you want to come with me?" His little face looks up at her, filled with hope.

"Sure thing," she says, after a quick glance at me to make sure it's okay.

Jacob scoots off the chair and runs from the veranda. At least he's holding the arm against his chest, but I wonder how well it's actually going to heal. Ellie follows close behind as they disappear around the corner of the house.

"It probably needs to be in a sling."

Alex nods but I don't think he's really listening to me. "Jacob was out of his mind last night in pain. He doesn't really know what he saw."

The creep-factor I always feel around Alex intensifies. I decide not to mention that Jacob said he saw Mason *before* he broke his arm. "Sure," I say casually. "Kids think they see things all the time but they're so busy doing other stuff they get it wrong."

The pinched look on Alex's face relaxes a little. "Exactly."

Jacob races back around the corner, eggs packed in a calico bag filled with straw. I wonder how many have broken on the rough trip back here. "Here you go, Kate. Thanks."

I smile at him. "Rest that arm, okay?"

"Sure."

I roll my eyes at him and he laughs. Oh, to be eight and too busy for pain to slow you down. Alex holds out his hand while Ellie packs the medic bag, and I only hesitate for a second before shaking it. Even though I want it to end as soon as it's started. Even though I wipe my hand on my shorts after.

"Thanks again for coming over. Let me know if there's anything we can do for you."

I hold up the eggs as I step off the veranda, Ellie beside me with the medic bag in her hands. "This is a great payment."

He shrugs. "Well, hopefully the boys will stay out

of trouble for long enough that we won't need to call you over again anytime soon."

"Hopefully." I give him a small wave, before walking down the path beside the huts.

I can feel Ellie's agitation on the walk back to our Territory. It's coming off her in waves, rolling into me, colliding with my own nervous tension. I want to say something . . . anything . . . to make her feel better but this definitely isn't the place to have this conversation.

I don't know what to say to her anyway. My thoughts are cascading through my mind, too quick to make sense of any of them, let alone make the pieces fit together. There's obviously something Alex knows about Mason. His reaction to Jacob's comment is too weird— too abrupt—to be a normal reaction. And yet, I still don't know what to make of it. The idea that a member of the Authority would deliberately injure Mason doesn't make any sense . . . none of it makes any sense.

A couple of people call to us as we make it back to our Territory and I wave and keep walking, not wanting to get caught in a conversation where I have to act normal. Hell, it doesn't even feel as if I'm walking normally. All I can think about is Mason's white face and Alex's reaction and the stab wound . . . and the feeling that it's starting all over again. All the unrest and fighting and not really knowing what I need to do to survive—

like we've gone back five years; even four years. I don't want to go back there. I just can't!

Gavin is waiting at the bottom of the terraces, close to the water, as we come over the hill. There's no way to avoid him and still get to the boat. I'm tempted to turn around but I know I need to act natural—do the things I always do—return the medic bag and not draw attention to myself. Everything's fine.

I stop as I come up to him. Ellie pushes past, moving down to the dinghy. It's probably for the best, even though selfishly, I would've enjoyed the backup. Gavin looks back at me, eyebrows raised, a clear question in his face.

"Women's problems." The words blurt out of my mouth before I can even think. Lame. But he seems to accept it and nods. I hold the eggs out to him—my movements feeling off... jarring almost. "We remembered."

He takes the bag. "Thanks. Good work." I go to walk past him, but he clears his throat as though he wants to say more. "Everyone okay up there?"

I nod stiffly. "Sure. Just a broken bone to fix."

He frowns at me, quiet for a moment. "Is everything okay?"

I try to smile. "Of course. Better get back to the boat. Ellie's waiting for me."

"Sure. Sure." But I can feel his eyes on me as I walk down to the boat. Shit! I *am* crap at this.

Ellie starts rowing before I'm even properly seated. "He knows something," she hisses, pulling on the oars like they've done something to personally insult her. "Alex, I mean."

"Yeah. I'm just not sure what it all means."

She bites her lip, looking up past me to the Territory. "Do you think Gavin knows something too?"

I shrug. "Who the hell knows with Gavin? He must have been a poker player before the Rise. He has the best poker face ever."

"Yeah."

And then, we're at the boat, climbing aboard, Ellie right on my heels as we step on the deck. I can hear a noise coming from inside, someone talking, and my heart plummets on its own personal slippery slide. God, oh God, has someone found Mason while we've been away?

I race into my cabin and then stop, staring at the scene in front of me. Mason is still lying on the floor, tangled in the sheets and covered in sweat. As I watch, he cries out, mumbles something, and then rolls over. I take a deep breath. No-one's discovered him, he's just been talking in his sleep. I'm grateful it's before midday and everyone's still over on the land. Well, hopefully.

"Mason." Reaching down, I touch his shoulder, but he doesn't wake. I gently brush my fingers across his forehead—he isn't hot, thank God, but it's too soon for a fever to set in, anyway. Lifting the covers a little, I check his wound. His movements have made the bandage come a little loose, but there's no fresh blood. I close my eyes and let out a long breath.

"Is he okay?" Ellie's voice is soft, almost a whisper.

"Yeah, I think he's dreaming. Probably understandable given what he's gone through."

My touch seems to have soothed him and he's quiet again, breathing evenly. My chest feels a little less constricted as I watch him. We've been friends for such a long time and he's been with me through all of it. Primary school, high school, teenage dramas, deciding what we want to do with our lives . . . and then, our world changing, destroying all of those carefully chosen dreams. We lost so many people we loved and yet we always had each other as we tried to make sense of our new lives.

Despite the fact I don't want to be back where we were five years ago—that the thought of more conflict has my whole system wanting to shut down, wanting to run and never stop—I know I need to protect him, just like he'd protect me if he needed to. I need to suck it up and do whatever I can to keep him safe.

I stand up and go back out to the main living area of the boat. Ellie's tapping her fingers against the porthole and I watch her for a second before making a decision.

"I need to try and work out what's happened. Now. Before anyone finds out Mason's here."

She stops tapping and turns to look at me. "How?"

"I'm going to find his boat. Jacob said he saw it from their Territory—so it must be hidden in one of the coves further along."

"But you can't leave the Territory without permission from the Authority."

"I know."

"I'll come with you."

"No."

She frowns but I don't give her time to talk.

"I need you to stay here with Mason, in case he gets loud again. And I need you to come out on the deck and go back inside again a few times over the next few hours, so everyone thinks we're both still over here, doing stuff."

She screws her face up, obviously not liking the idea but then sighs. "Okay."

I'm a bit shocked she's agreed so easily. Not that I'm going to point that out to her. "And I'm going to need your kayak."

"It's still over behind the shed."

"I'll have to swim over and hope no one sees me."

She snorts and I put my hands on my hips.

"What?"

"Just, you know, your ability to be sneaky is almost as bad as your ability to tell a lie." She grins at me.

I arch one eyebrow. "I'm plenty sneaky."

"Sure, sure. Whatever you say."

I know she's trying to make me feel better—make both of us feel better—and I smile at her, trying to keep a tight grip on my taught nerves at the same time. I don't want to do this, even though I know I have to.

"I'll be back as quickly as I can."

Ellie nods and I turn, going before I change my mind. The boat faces away from the land and I crouch down low, hurrying to the front—away from prying eyes—and lower myself into the waiting ocean, thankful it's warm. I swim slowly, trying to be quiet as I go behind all the boats, praying no one's come back for any reason, but waiting, waiting, for someone to see me and call out. To ask what I'm doing. And I can't think of a lie I can tell, no matter how much I try. After what seems like hours but is probably only ten minutes, I'm at the edge of our Territory, behind the big shed where we house our supplies and equipment and have our Territory meetings.

I crouch down again as I wade out of the water, leaving wet footprints behind me, and move quickly to Ellie's kayak. Grabbing it, I secure it under my arm, holding the paddle under the other, heart pounding, expecting any moment that someone's going to come around the end of the shed and find me.

But it never comes. And I'm back in the water, paddling as quietly as I can out behind the boats of Territory Two, following the curve of the land, mouth so dry with the fear of being seen I keep swallowing to try and get some moisture happening. God, I would've totally sucked as a spy.

It takes another fifteen minutes to get past Territory Two and then I'm even with the Authority's main building, sitting on its own—a solid, brick house, abandoned after the Rise, looking out over the ocean. A view it was never supposed to have. Who knows what happened to the original owners, but Carl took it for the main building when he first settled the Territories—land that hadn't yet been claimed by anyone else. The survival instinct that kicked in for so many after the Rise meant that people at the top of the mountains weren't willing to share, and the fighting that followed is still burned in my brain.

Carl was the one who pulled us all together. He

found the land, he brought us together as a group—a motley collection of waifs . . . lost survivors—and organised us to protect our claim. Carl—and the rest of the Authority that maintain order in the Territories—are the reason we even have a home.

That's what makes Mason's plea not to tell the Authority even more confusing. More painful. Surely it couldn't be an Authority member who hurt him . . .

I move past the Authority building as fast as I can, praying no one is looking out the windows, holding my breath as if that's going to hide me in some way out here on the endless ocean. Eventually, I'm parallel with the land that's been split off from our Territories, deemed not suitable for settlement because it's way too steep—the mountains leaving little purchase to even attempt to terrace it.

I paddle harder, making sure not to use the side of Ellie's paddle with the crack, less on guard now, when I come to a natural inlet. And then I see it. Mason's boat, anchored so it's not noticeable until you're at the entrance.

Bringing the kayak to a stop, I sit as silently as I can, trying to slow my breathing, waiting to see if anyone's around. I hear the gentle lap of water against the kayak, the sound of insects and the occasional bird flying high overhead. I poise my paddle, ready to turn at the slightest hint of company. After five minutes, I move slowly forward, coming up to the back of the boat and the ladder hanging into the water. Tying the kayak to the boat, I climb on board. No one comes out to inspect the noise and I let out a breath I didn't realise I was holding.

I glance around, not even sure what I'm looking for. There's a dark stain on the deck in front of me and I bend down, looking at it. Blood. Blood soaked into the wood. I can't see anything he might have fallen onto, so the idea that he was stabbed deliberately seems more and more probable.

"What have you got yourself into?" I murmur under my breath.

If Mason anchored the boat over here, away from Territory One, without permission from the Authority, then he's in trouble. The boundaries between the Territories are strict, and this area is definitely a no-go zone. Why would he be over here? Was he doing something wrong and got found out . . . but that's not the Mason I know. It can't be.

Or was he stabbed when he was moored somewhere else, and then whoever did it moved the boat around here afterwards? Moved it so we wouldn't know Mason was back . . . and we'd all believe he'd never returned. That we'd lost him to this new world we lived in with its sudden, ferocious storms and hazards waiting just under the water from our wrecked civilization.

It was only luck that I found him floating, almost dead . . .

I shake my head. I can't waste time. I need to look and get back before anyone gets suspicious. I go down into the cabin. It's meticulous, as always. I tease Mason about how pedantic he is, keeping everything in order— in its place. The logbook is on the desk to the side of the cabin and I rub my hand over the green cover before opening it up. There, in his neat handwriting, are the details of his last trip. He'd gone south, as far as what used to be Brisbane city by the looks of it. And then there's a notation I don't understand.

7S. 4F. 3M.

The strange letters and numbers are followed by co-ordinates—a place, I assume, where he found something. Something he wanted to be able to get back to? Or something he wanted to keep secret? Did he find something worth being stabbed over? Shit. It doesn't help me at all!

I slam the book closed and look around again. Nothing is out of place. Nothing's been disturbed. It's as if everything is fine—normal. Except Mason is still unconscious on my floor with a stab wound.

THE RISE

I hit the wall with the palm of my hand in frustration. There are no answers here, just more questions. And I need to get back. Leaving the logbook on the desk—I don't want to raise suspicions by removing it—I make my way onto the deck and untie the kayak. The sun's high in the sky and I can feel it beating down on me as I make my way back past the Authority building and the boats in Territory Two. It must be past midday and people will be stopping for lunch, looking out over the water . . .

It's Gavin who sees me. He's holding a hoe and looks up just as I'm between boats, shading his eyes with his hands as he looks over the water. There's no way he hasn't seen me. Shit. Shit. Triple shit. Thankfully, I've already crossed the threshold back into Territory One—that's something, at least.

My mind whirls, thoughts crashing into each other as I try to come up with a decent reason as to why I'm out in the kayak. Because there's no way he's not going to ask me what I was doing. Christ, I'm so bad at this!

Ellie's boat. It's behind me. I can say I've been there, getting . . . something.

I paddle quickly back to my boat and secure the kayak before climbing aboard. Ellie meets me out on the deck.

"He saw me. Gavin. He saw me coming back."

Ellie looks over to the shore, her eyes narrowed. "Do you think he'll come over?"

I shrug, feeling panicky. "I don't know. Maybe. Or he'll wait for us to go back over there. I think he only saw me once I'd reached our Territory. I just need a good reason . . . oh!" I breathe a sigh of relief as a thought dawns on me.

Ellie's eyes narrow. "What?"

"I told him you had your period when we came back from Three. Sorry. But we can say I was over at your boat getting supplies."

Ellie's frown turns to a grin. "At least he won't ask a lot of questions then."

I smile back. It feels forced. "Yeah, that's what I'm hoping."

"Mason's still out of it. Did you find his boat?"

"Yeah, but . . . there were more questions than answers." I think of the strange notation in the logbook and the coordinates underneath. "I'll tell you about it later."

"Okay. Should we go back on land so no-one comes over here?"

I want to say no. I don't want to go over and invite the questions but it's stupid and naïve to think they won't come. "Yes. We should."

We leave Ellie's kayak at the boat and she joins me in the dinghy. Gavin's waiting for us as we pull into shore. And he's not the only one. Alex is there with him.

I struggle not to show the panic I'm feeling on my face. I don't know if I'm successful because neither of them look happy. "Hey, Alex. What are you doing over here? Is Jacob all right?"

He smiles at me. It doesn't make me feel any better. "He's fine. I just thought I'd come over and tell Gavin in person what a great job you did this morning."

"Oh. Well, thanks."

He nods, as if I should be eternally grateful he honoured me by taking the time out to do this, and I feel my mouth tighten.

"Yes." Gavin's watching us both. "It was nice of you to come all this way when I'm sure you've got work to do."

Alex smiles again, like Gavin's making a joke rather than having a not so subtle dig, and throws his arm around our rep's shoulders. Gavin doesn't look comfortable, but he doesn't move away either.

"Well, you know how it is. It's a positive thing to build feelings of goodwill between the Territories. In fact, I was over chatting to Rosa in Territory Two about half an hour ago."

My heart feels like it's trying to escape my chest

cavity and I wipe my palms on my shorts. Half an hour ago, when I would have been paddling by . . . "Really?" I force the word out of my mouth. "And how is Rosa?"

"Good. Good. I told her about your work too. She was impressed." A smile tugs at his lips.

Now I know he's lying. Rosa, the Authority rep for Two has never liked me. And two months ago, when she refused to ask for medical assistance for a Territory Two woman having a difficult labour, the hatred intensified. The poor people lost their baby and I know I could've helped. I didn't hold back in telling her—yelling at her actually—and she hasn't forgiven me. Probably never will. She's that sort of person.

There's silence again. I wait for one of them to break it—to ask me what I was doing out on the kayak. But neither speaks.

Ellie—bless her—pushes past them. "Well, I'm sure we've all got work to do. Kate's going to show me how to make a herb bunch that'll help with menstrual pains. God, I hate being a woman sometimes."

I choke on my laughter at the look on both of their faces and take Ellie's lead, moving past both of them. I think I'm in the clear, already stepping up to the first terrace when Alex calls out my name. I don't want to turn—I want to pretend I haven't heard him—but my steps falter and I know I have to.

I turn slowly. He's watching me.

"I was saying to Gavin it'd be great to know when Mason gets back. There's some things I need to talk to him about."

He watches me closely, and I make sure to keep my face neutral, to resist the impulse to look at my boat. "Of course," I say, turning back to the terrace. My hands shake. There was a clear threat in Alex's voice and I know without a doubt that he had something to do with Mason's stabbing.

CHAPTER THREE

I can't take the chance of going back to the boat for the rest of the afternoon. It'd look too suspicious. Alex leaves shortly after he speaks to me, but Gavin watches us all afternoon, as if he's trying to work something out. Or waiting to catch me out . . .

But he still doesn't say anything as we come down from the herb garden. Ellie and I chat with some of the other residents—friendly, normal, nothing strange going on. I don't notice any weird looks shot my way, so I guess we're successful.

We are both quiet on the way back over to the boat, lost in our thoughts. It's hard to put one hand after the other to climb up on deck and I just want to crawl into my bunk and forget everything. I want to wake up to see Mason back from his trip, uninjured, knowing I have nothing to worry about.

"I think I might go back to my boat," Ellie says. "I'll just grab my bag from inside."

I nod at her, too tired to ask her to stay, and we go inside.

Inside to see Mason.

Who's awake and sitting at my table.

He smiles, but it's not the big Mason smile I'm used to. It's one that shows he nearly died this morning. The big bruise coming out on his cheek probably isn't helping that image.

"Hey."

I move closer. "Hey. How are you feeling?"

"I don't know." He rubs his hands through his hair. "Tired. Sore."

Ellie moves past me and stands next to his seat, looking at him for a moment, her brown eyes serious, before leaning down and throwing her arms around him. He hugs her back until she stands up and whacks him on the arm.

"Ouch!"

"That's for nearly dying on us."

He chuckles. "Yeah. I'll try not to do it again."

"You'd better not."

I sit on the chair on the other side of the table and he leans forward, putting his hand over mine.

"Thanks, Katie girl, for rescuing me this morning. You don't know how glad I am you're an early riser."

I feel the tears in my eyes and try to blink them away, try to breathe and think and not overreact. He's okay. He's alive. I turn my hand over, squeezing his.

"What happened? Your side . . . Were you stabbed?" I can hear the emotion in my voice and take another breath.

Mason hesitates, glancing over at Ellie, protectiveness clear on his face, and she squeezes her lips tight.

"Don't even think about leaving me out of this. I'm not a kid and you're my friend."

"Ellie . . ." His face looks pained. I wonder if I had the same look when I tried to talk her into staying out of it. No wonder it didn't work.

"Don't 'Ellie' me, Mason. Just don't, okay?"

He looks to me for support and I shrug. "Already tried it. Didn't work for me either."

He rubs his hand through his hair again and sighs. "Yeah, I was stabbed."

And even though I was already pretty sure that's what happened, the confirmation skewers my chest, making it ache. "By who?"

"Members of the Authority." His eyes look hard. Like he can't believe the words coming out of his mouth.

I can't either. My brain refuses to believe it's possible, even if I know Mason would never lie about this. Christ. My heart's pounding, trying to free itself of the constriction of my ribs and I want to get up and walk away. Pretend it's not happening. But I don't. I take a deep breath and try and get my thoughts in order instead.

"Was Alex one of them?" Ellie's eyes are as hard as Mason's.

He looks up at her and then nods.

"I knew it!" She slaps her hand on her thigh. "I knew he was a douchebag."

I barely hear what Ellie says. I'm still staring at Mason, watching his face like it'll give me answers. He looks back at me and gives me a half smile, as if I'm the one who needs supporting, rather than him.

The shock—the dread of what's to come—must show on my face. "Why would he hurt you? Try to kill you?"

In my head, I'm back there. Back when the survivors—those of us who were lucky enough to survive the initial Rise—turned on each other. Fighting over resources and land and stupid things that meant nothing but seemed suddenly really, really important.

In some ways, the violence of those first few

years affected me more than losing people in the Rise. At least that wasn't a choice—we had no control over it, it was simply Mother Nature removing a few million of her inhabitants. But when people starting killing each other, *that* was horrifying.

I'd spent a lot of my time trying to save people who'd been attacked by other human beings for food or water or land. Spent each day feeling sad and scared and horrified and angry, watching people bleed out and stop breathing in my arms. People who'd survived the decimation of our world but hadn't survived human greed until Carl set up of the Authority—our tiny government in a changed world—and gave us some order with the Territories.

I shake my head, as if that's going to get rid of the images I can still see plainly, like I'm back there again. And maybe I am. If the Authority are going around stabbing people . . . stabbing *Mason*.

My fingers shake and Mason grips my hand again. I focus on his touch, on the feel of the seat underneath me, drawing in oxygen until I feel I can breathe normally. God, will I ever get over this? Will it ever stop and let me be the Kate I was before? I'm scared the answer will be no.

"You okay?" I can see the concern in his eyes.

"Yes. Thanks." I give his hand one last squeeze

and then lean back. "So, what happened?"

He rubs his eyes. "It's a long story."

"We've got all night."

"I'm staying too," says Ellie, as if there's any doubt.

"Fair enough." Mason sighs and then grimaces. "God, I'm not even sure where to start. You know when I headed off a week ago, I was planning to go north to do some diving and scavenging?"

I frown at him. "But you went south?"

His face goes still. "How did you know that?"

"I found your boat," I say, sitting up straighter. "And I looked at the log."

"Jesus, Katie!" He stands but it must hurt because he winces and sits down again. "I can't believe you did that. Do you know how much danger you've put yourself in? God, if anything had happened to you, I wouldn't have been . . . God!"

"I had to try to work out what was happening," I say, my voice heated. I'm not sure if it's in defence of myself or in response to the emotion in his voice. "You were almost dead in the water. Stabbed. If I hadn't found you . . ."

"Shh," says Ellie, and I know she's right—voices carry across the water.

I shake my head, lowering my voice. "I had to

know. In case they found you."

"Yeah but Katie, please, you need—"

"Mason, stop. Just tell us what happened."

He sighs again, like I'm being a pain the arse. "Yes, I went south. There was some bad weather coming in up north. I told Gavin and he was okay with the change so I went down to the old Brisbane city area. There are still some buildings there that haven't been completely searched, so I thought it might be a good opportunity to scavenge them."

"Did you find anything good?"

He turns to Ellie and gives a small smile. "Well, I found you a new paddle."

They high five each other but I'm too strung out to join in their celebration.

"And then what happened?"

The smile slips off his face. "I decided to go further into the city. I wanted to make more notations on my map of the submerged buildings and debris so it'd be easier to get in and out in the future. I was diving, searching through stuff, and then there was this building. I think it was close to where the river had been, still upright, but the concrete underneath wasn't looking great. It didn't look like it was going to last much longer."

I think of trips to Brisbane before the Rise, trying to picture the buildings Mason is talking about. I can imagine what the salt water and the tides and the storms have done to them now. Mother Nature is trying her best to wipe out evidence of our existence. Just as well we're a tenacious species.

"I went back to the boat and then found the building again. It looked like someone had gone through it before but there were still some good things there. I loaded stuff up and then took some other things down to one of the units closer to the water line, to come back and get it later."

He takes a deep breath and shifts, his wound obviously causing him pain.

"Do you need anything?" I get up to sort through my medic bag.

"Sit down, Katie. I'm fine."

I stop and sit down again, watching him. This feels like the big part of the story and now we're here, I don't know that I want to hear it. Not because I'm a coward. At least I hope not. But I've enjoyed the routine of the last few years. The normality. And I really want to hang on to that. Stupid.

Mason takes my hand, running his hand across my knuckles, as if he knows what I'm thinking. "I went up to the top floor and the door up there was jammed. I thought there might be some good things in there if no one else had made it in, so I grabbed a piece of wood and started bashing into it. But before I could get through, it opened."

"What?" I sit forward, confused.

"Who was it?" Ellie eyes are wide, absorbed in the story.

"It was a family. A family who'd lived there since the Rise!"

I open my mouth and then shut it again, not knowing what to say. How could someone have survived for five years in a half-submerged building? On their own? There are pirates happy to take whatever they can; attack whoever they can. That's part of the reason we'd formed Territories—for protection. How had this family hidden for so long?

"A family?"

"Yep. Seven of them. Four females and three males."

I blinked. "The code in your log. That's what it stands for. Seven survivors."

He smiles. "Yep. And they were in a bad way. I thought they were going to shoot me at first. One of them had a gun. A gun! But when I explained I wasn't going to hurt them, they let me in."

"Holy crap." I lean back. "I can hardly believe they survived for five years. Did they have a boat?"

He shakes his head. "No. They've been fishing

from the building apparently. And in the penthouse, they've got an outside area, so they have a garden going. Enough to feed the seven of them as well as raiding the other units for food over the years. But no way to get off. And they've got two little kids. One's only about three, so born after the Rise."

I shake my head at the thought—having to give birth without any help apart from what your family can offer you would be scary. "How've they stayed hidden?"

"Cheng, he's the dad, said there's been a couple of times when they thought the pirates were going to find them but they were prepared."

"Prepared? How?"

He raises his eyebrows. "It was unbelievable. The house is full of weapons. Guns, swords—crazy stuff. Apparently, he was a weapons importer and specialist before the Rise and they used part of the apartment as a storeroom."

"Wow. Gavin would kill for some of that." And then I realise what I've said and cover my mouth with my hand. "Oh my God. Was it Gavin?"

Mason's eyes are hard. "No. Gavin wasn't part of it. I don't think so anyway."

"What happened then?"

"The family—the Li's—they asked me to bring them back here. To the Territories. They wanted to be able to settle their family on land; get medical help. The Grandmother's in a really bad way. I told them they could come back with me but they wouldn't be able to get off the boat until they were given the all clear. That I needed to get the approval of the Authority."

I nod. That's the rule. Even people who find us over land aren't allowed to enter the Territories until they've had interviews and been given the okay. But if they're sick . . . surely it would be okay. Surely . . .

"But they didn't want to move the Grandma until they knew for certain. She's so frail. And they didn't want to split up. I told them I'd be back in three days. Four at the most. I thought I could get you to come, Katie, see if you could help the Grandma before we moved her."

"Of course."

"Cheng offered me all their weapons—everything. You wouldn't believe what they've got stored there. Weapons we could use to protect the Territories, and all this gold and jewellery. Stuff we could trade. He offered all of it if we let them in. I told him he didn't need to but he's adamant he wants to pay his way."

I shift in my seat, tucking my hands under my legs. "What was the problem then? Why'd the Authority try and kill you?"

His rubs the back of his neck. "I went straight to the Authority house when I got here. I just wanted to get things organised as soon as possible for the family. It was late but Carl called a special meeting of the reps, although not everyone came. Gavin wasn't there and neither was Kathy from Five or Sue from Four."

"Who was there?"

"Alex. Rosa. Zack from Nine, Lisa from Seven and Chris from Six. They were all arguing. Arguing about whether we should let any more people in. People who didn't have skills that we needed here. Especially people not . . . local."

"What? Because they're from the city?"

Mason raises an eyebrow.

"Because they're Chinese?"

He nods and I can't help the snort that comes out.

"God, I thought we'd left that shit behind after the Rise. I can't believe it."

"But why stab *you*?" Ellie asks. "Why would they do that?"

Mason grips my hand hard. Hard enough to hurt. But I don't pull away. He needs me to be strong for him. "They wanted me to go back and take all the stuff. The weapons. The jewellery. They didn't want the family here but said we had the right to everything they offered."

"Just take it from the family? And not help them? Like a pirate?"

He nods. "But that wasn't the worst of it. They said if I needed to, I should kill them. Chris and Lisa were against that but the rest weren't. They were going on and on about shit stuff, like survival of the fittest, and protecting the Territories from outsiders. Alex was a big one for that. He was pretty adamant I should do whatever I needed to get the weapons and bring them back."

"What? Are you serious?"

"Yes." One simple word.

I can see the truth in his eyes. Even if I'd rather not believe it, I have to.

"He wanted you to kill innocent people? Survivors?" I feel like I'm going to be sick. People I know—people I've helped and trusted—are happy to kill a whole family because they have stuff we want? It doesn't feel real.

"I told them I wouldn't do it. That it was wrong. That we needed to bring this family back and offer them a home, a safe place. But they wouldn't listen." The words come quickly, rushing out of Mason's mouth now, like they can't be held back any longer. "They kept arguing though, yelling over each other. It was crazy, what they were saying. Terrible. As if I didn't know them anymore. But the one who actually held the knife—that tried to kill me . . ." He glances at Ellie, a sad look on his face. "Well, it was Carl."

THE RISE

Ellie gasps, her face white. Carl's her surrogate grandfather—the man who saved her after the Rise. He found her on the island, brought her back to the mainland, held her when she cried and cried about losing her whole family.

She shakes her head, eyes wide. "No. No, no, no. You've got it wrong. Maybe you're not remembering it right. If everyone was there, and with you losing blood and everything, you must've been confused or something. It can't have been Carl."

Mason goes to touch her arm but she draws back, away from him. He sighs.

"I'm sorry, Ellie. It was Carl."

"It was an accident then." Her voice is high-pitched and I'm reminded of how young she is. "He didn't mean to hurt you. It was just an accident."

Mason shakes his head and I watch her face fall. "Everyone was arguing and yelling and Carl said he wanted to have a quiet word with me. So I went with him."

"I don't understand." I can hear the sadness in Ellie's voice; her disbelief. "Why? Why would he hurt you?"

"We went back to the boat," he says. "I thought he was going to tell me to bring the family back and we'd sort it out. Tell me he didn't agree with what the others were saying. Be a good leader." Mason reaches out to take Ellie's hand, but she pulls away again, tears running down her face.

"He *is* a good leader." But she's lost all conviction in her voice.

"He wanted to know how much the family had," continues Mason, "and how easily I could take it from them. When I told him I wouldn't do it, he asked me for the co-ordinates, told me he'd get someone who would. I refused, saying I'd get there first and grab the family and let the people of the Territories make the decision—tell them what the members of the Authority were asking me to do. It was probably a stupid thing to say, in hindsight." Mason smiles without humour. "He told me he couldn't let me do that. And then he stabbed me. Even apologised for doing it." He laughs and it isn't a nice one. "He stabbed me and dragged me to the side of my own boat. Pushed me over. And then he took the dinghy back to the house. And he just left me. Left me to die."

His voice is a whisper at the end and I put my other hand over his, gripping it between both of mine. I want to rush out and scream at all the members of the Authority. Make them pay for their decision. But that won't help. Not yet.

"I tried to stay afloat, to get back to shore, except I got caught up in a current, and I was losing so much blood . . . Thank God you found me."

Ellie stands up straight, her face a tight mask, trying to hold everything in. "We'll take you on shore. Show everyone your wound—tell them what the Authority did to you."

Mason shakes his head. "It's their word against mine, six to one—and six Authority voices are a lot more trustworthy than one scavenger."

"We need to get to the family, then," says Ellie. "God, they might have already sent someone to kill them! We need to get there. Get there before . . ." She doesn't say his name. "We should leave now."

Mason's shaking his head before she's even finished talking. "*I'll* go and get them, Ellie. Me and Kate, because I need her medical experience, otherwise I wouldn't ask her to come either. It's too dangerous. I'd never forgive myself if anything happened to either of you."

"I'm not a child!" she says, slapping her hand on the benchtop. "I wish people would stop treating me like one."

"I know you're not. I know! But you can do more good for us if you stay here. Tell them Katie's not well— that she's contagious or something and you're staying here to look after her until she's better. Delay them following us, if you can. But only if you can. They already think I'm dead so they need a reason for Kate not being available."

"Alex's already suspicious of me," I say quietly. "He saw me kayaking out beyond Territory Two."

"Shit!" says Mason. "We need to get you out of here."

Ellie looks torn, as if she can understand what Mason's saying but still doesn't like it—still doesn't want to agree. Finally, she sighs. "Fine. I'll tell them you're sick," she says, looking at me. "But you both better come back. Otherwise, I'll be really shitty!"

I go over to give her a hug and she holds on to my shirt for a moment, like she's afraid to let go.

"We'll come back. I promise."

She steps back and nods. "When are you going to leave?"

"Tonight," Mason says, wincing as he stands. "We'll go while it's dark."

CHAPTER FOUR

The fact that the moon hasn't yet risen means the darkness is almost complete. It's one of the things that took a lot of getting used to after the Rise—the lack of light from towns and cities. Our world has become darker.

Mason's boat cuts through the water, sails full, as we make our way south. It was still in the inlet when we'd got there, thank God. I'd been worried that members of the Authority—or whoever they were going to send after the family—might've taken it during the afternoon. But then, if someone else had seen Mason's boat without him on it, it would've taken some explaining.

I do the physical work of setting the sails, but

Mason looks better now he's doing something. He's always enjoyed being on the water; it was something he shared with his family growing up—sailing, fishing, diving—that's why he'd chosen to fish and scavenge for the Territory. Even though he's told me he misses me when he's away, I know he loves the solitary life it gives him. Time away from the Territory. Time away from everyone watching, making sure you're pulling your weight.

We've been best friends for so long—reliant on each other for support both before and after the Rise—I can't imagine him not being in my life. The thought of him not being here, never seeing him again . . . my stomach twists and squeezes, and I want to go and wrap him in my arms and kiss him in a way that feels decidedly not best-friend-ish.

I've felt this way before—just before the Rise, we'd been spending more time together than usual, going out, exploring different places . . . And I'd started to think of him as maybe more than a friend. God knows if he did—I was pretty good at hiding my feelings from him, not sure what it'd do to our friendship. Not sure if I was ready to take the risk. And then the world went unrecognisably insane and I wasn't sure of anything anymore, let alone how I felt.

But now . . . well, all the feelings from before the

Rise seem to have come back one hundredfold.

I shake my head. Not something I should be thinking about at this point in time. God. Head in the game, Kate. Get a grip!

Mason hauls himself up to the front of the deck and I watch him closely. I'd refused to let him row us over to his boat earlier and he'd given in so quickly, I knew he was still really sore. He sits down next to me and leans back, looking up at the stars.

"It's amazing when you think about it," he says. "So much has changed down here—so many people lost—and yet, up there, everything's still the same. The stars the sailors would've used to navigate hundreds of years ago are still the ones we're using now."

I smile, leaning back with him. "Why, Mason Grey, you're a poet."

He grins at me for a moment before his smile fades away and he looks back at the sky. "I can't believe they did what they did, you know. The Authority. Carl."

I take a deep breath. "What happens when we get back?"

"Honestly, I don't know. I just know I can't let those people die. Even if the Authority doesn't kill them, that building's close to collapsing. We need to help them."

"Do you think everyone will feel the same? I

mean, there are people in the Territories from all different cultures. Surely they'll be okay to welcome this family?"

He sighs. "I hope so. I think so. But the Grandma's a liability—"

I start to protest, but Mason talks over me.

"I'm not saying it's right, I'm just saying she's a liability, if you put yourself into the mindset of before. We need people who have skills, people who can pull their weight . . . She's sick, and they have young children too. More mouths to feed." He sighs. "I *hope* our community will welcome them anyway. Just because we should. They're survivors, like us. But maybe more people than I expect will think the same as the Authority."

I touch his arm and he takes my hand in his, our fingers entwining in a way that feels right. My heart's being turned inside out with the uncertainty of whether he feels the same. I push the thought out of my head, focusing instead on our hands touching, the sound of the waves on the boat . . .

We sit there in comfortable silence, watching the water and the stars and I try not to think about what'll be waiting for us when we get back.

If we get back.

We make it to where the Port of Brisbane used to

be by eight the next night and anchor up, Mason not willing to sail the treacherous waters until we have sunlight to help us see submerged obstacles. He knows where most of them are but bits of buildings, drowned trees and vestiges of the old world continue to break off and create new hazards.

As I pull the sails down, Mason moves into the cabin and I follow him, looking forward to a few hours rest before we have to move again. He's in the galley as I come down the steps, a smile on his face, hands behind his back.

"I've got a surprise for you."

I narrow my eyes. Mason's always been a practical joker and I've learnt from past experience not to be too trusting. But then, he brings his hands around and I gasp, a shiver of delight coursing through my body—such a small thing to create such a big reaction.

"Oh my God! Really. Where did you find them?"

I take the packet from him and clutch it my chest. A whole unopened packet of Wagon Wheels. No doubt they'll be stale but I don't care. They were my go-to comfort food when I was a teenager. My go-to anything, really. And seeing the packet brings back so many memories, my eyes start to tear up. Mason grabs me in a hug, the packet of biscuits between us.

"Oh, Katie-girl, I didn't mean to make you cry!"

I shake my head, laughing as tears drip down my face. "No, no, it's okay. They're great. The best present ever. Thank you."

He stands back slightly, hands still on my arms, looking at me, before leaning down and kissing me—a kiss so unexpected, it takes me a moment to respond. And then I do and he's kissing me harder, his arms around my back, pulling me in again. We're both breathless when we break apart.

He runs the back of his fingers down my cheek. "You know, all I could think of, when I was in the water, feeling my strength ebbing away, was how I'd never get a chance to do that."

I run my thumb over his lips. "I'm happy you did."

And he kisses me again.

In this moment, everything is perfect in my world. Even though there are things we have yet to face—even though I don't know how tomorrow is going to go—at this moment, in this space, my world is good. Good enough that I'm even happy to share the chocolate marshmallow goodness of the Wagon Wheels.

CHAPTER FIVE

As the sun peeks over the horizon behind us, we sail into
Brisbane. I stand at the bow of the boat, watching for
submerged obstacles, although Mason knows what he's
doing. He's done it enough times to know where most of
them are and his charts are pedantically filled in. Still, it's
better to be safe than sorry. And it gives me something
else to do, other than constantly look behind us, checking
the horizon for another boat. So far, there hasn't been
one and there's a small bubble of hope in me that maybe,
just maybe, we might be able to get in and get the family
out without a confrontation.

It's another hour and a half before we make it to
the building. Mason uses some of our precious fuel for

the last five minutes to get us closer when the wind fails us. The fuel should give us a quick get-away—although we're hoping we won't need one.

Rather than feeling more settled, the closer we get to the building, the more on-edge I feel, like the blood in my system is slowly being replaced by adrenalin. My hands are shaking so much, it takes me three attempts to untie the dinghy and, once we're in it, I can't row fast enough.

Finally, finally, we're at the building where Mason found the family. He ties our small boat to the frame of one of the windows that's already lost its glass and we climb through the window. I look back at Mason, heart forgetting its proper rhythm for a moment, as he gasps, his hands going to his side, pain evident on his face.

"Are you okay?" My voice is quiet. I don't know why, except it's hard to not feel like we're being watched.

He nods, leaning against the wall, breathing hard. "Yeah. My muscles didn't appreciate having to pull me through the window."

I move closer and touch his arm. "That's because they haven't had a chance to heal. Do you want me to take a look?"

He attempts a smile. "No. Let's keep going. I'll be fine."

I want to disagree with him, keep him safe, but

we don't have that option.

Not yet.

I look back out the window. The water flowing around the building is still empty. We have time, even if my heart and adrenal system don't believe that. I hoist the medic bag further up my shoulder and turn back to Mason. "Can you keep going or do you want to stay here?"

He straightens, but it's clearly an effort. Like he's forcing himself. "I'm good. Let's get upstairs and let the Li's know we're here."

Taking my hand, he leads the way up, calling out as we climb higher in the building, dodging around discarded objects and startling birds who've made homes in the skeletal remains of the city. By the time we get to the top, I can see Mason's energy waning, and put my arm around his waist, giving him support.

He knocks on the door.

"Cheng. It's me. Mason. Open up."

I hear the clicking of locks and then the door opens a fraction and I can see an eye looking out at us through the crack. Then the door shuts again, there is a clatter as the chain slides across, and then it opens fully. A thin Chinese man smiles at Mason, the relief clear in his eyes.

"You came back for us?"

Mason nods. "Of course. I told you I would."

The man's eyes go down to my arm around Mason and the support I'm offering, before they flit up to me and then back to Mason.

"You are okay?"

Mason starts to nod and then hesitates, shaking his head instead. "No. But I told you I'd come and get you and your family, so here we are. This is Kate. She's a medic in our Territory. I thought she might be able to help your mother."

Cheng looks at me and bows slightly. "Welcome. Please, come in."

He lets us through the door and then turns, shutting it behind us before systematically working his way through three locks plus a door chain. I'm beginning to understand how they've remained hidden for so long.

The room he leads us through has a shabby but opulent feel to it. A slight woman with prominent cheekbones stands with two young children in the lounge room, wariness in her eyes as she watches us. Her hands grip the upper arms of the children, as if she's waiting to whisk them away if we prove untrustworthy. Beside her, a young man with a rifle in his hands follows us with his eyes, no expressions on his face. And even though the gun's still pointed at the floor, I can feel the threat in the air. They aren't taking any chances.

"Mrs Li," Mason says, nodding his head to her.

The woman nods back but doesn't say anything.

Mason turns to the boy with the rifle. "An, it's good to see you again."

The young man jerks his chin at Mason but he doesn't smile or look relieved.

"Is your mother okay?" I ask, turning to Cheng.

His face settles into a look of sadness. "No. She is weak. She is saying it's her time to go."

Mason looks at me and then to Cheng. "Cheng, listen. You know I told you I had to ask our Authority if we could settle you on our land?"

Cheng nods. "Yes, we have much of the weapons and jewellery ready for you to take."

Mason grimaces. "Well, there's been a bit of a change of plans. We're going to take you all back with us but you're going to leave all the stuff here. And we need to leave quickly. Soon. Very soon."

I can see the confusion on Cheng's face. "But your Territory would like it if we could bring these resources. It would help us be able to stay."

"Yes, I know." Mason runs his hand through his hair and the movement lifts his shirt slightly. Enough that they can see the bandage wrapped around his torso.

Cheng steps forward. "Someone hurt you?"

Mason pulls his shirt back down, a grimace on his

face. "Yes. The people in our Authority . . ." He stops and shakes his head. "Well, they don't want to let you in. They just want the stuff you have. But I told them we couldn't do that."

"They want you to take it from us, don't they?"

Cheng's calm acceptance—the lack of emotion in his voice—makes me wonder what he'd experienced before the Rise; what sort of life he lived. Not that it matters now. Now it's just important to get them away, make them safe. Give them a chance at a new life—a right every survivor of the Rise should have.

"Yes." Mason's voice is grim. "But I promised I'd help your family and I will. We're going to take you back and let the people of our Territory decide. I know they'll make the right decision. Or if you don't want that, I can take you wherever you want to go."

The younger man, An, goes to say something but Cheng holds up his hand, stopping him. He looks at Mason, eyes hard, staring, like he's trying to read his mind. Finally, he nods his head.

"I believe you are an honourable man. My family and I have nowhere else to go and I don't wish to have them homeless, wandering the land, not knowing who we might encounter or what they will do to us. Especially with my mother sick. We will try our luck with you and your Territory."

Mason lets out a relieved sigh. "Good. We need to get moving then. The Authority might be sending someone else to . . . take what they want."

Cheng nods, all action now. He grabs another rifle from the cupboard in the hallway and gestures to An. "You will watch for any others coming. Ming, get the children ready. Pack quickly."

His wife ushers the children out of the room, her eyes wide as she glances back at us. Afraid. Guilt wells up in me, even though I haven't done anything—would never agree with what the Authority want. Maybe it's just guilt that they have to be subjected to this vileness.

"Come," Cheng says, looking at me. "I will take you to my mother."

He takes me down a hallway to the left, Mason behind me. The old woman lying on the bed looks so tiny it's as if she's fading away to nothing. There's a young girl sitting beside her, maybe twelve or thirteen, who gets up as we enter the room.

"Yu," Cheng says, smiling at her. "Go help your aunt get the children ready and pack your own bag. We will leave soon."

The young girl looks at us with a small smile, her face hopeful, and runs out of the room. My heart aches for her. She's probably only a little older than Ellie was when she was found and even though Yu's not on her own, everything in me twists and knots at the life she must have had since the Rise. I want to get her away from this building so she and her family can start again. Have a life. I hope we get a chance to offer her that.

I kneel down beside the bed, smoothing the covers gently with my hand—not that they need it but it helps to settle my nerves. The old lady's brown eyes look at me steadily and I smile at her.

"My name's Kate. How are you feeling?"

Her eyes flick from me to her son and he speaks rapidly to her in Chinese. She speaks a few words back, her voice weary.

"She says she is sore all over and tired."

"Has she been eating?" I ask him.

"She has. A little. But none of us have been eating very well for at least a few months. A storm took a lot of our garden and it has not yet recovered."

I nod, understanding first-hand the frustration and despair at the damage the storms can wreak in only a few minutes. I smile gently at her before taking a piece of willow bark from my pack and handing it to her. Her hand is so tiny, I feel like a giant next to her.

"Can you tell your mother she needs to chew this? It should help with her pain. Enough that it will hopefully make the journey easier. And then, when we get to the Territories, we can feed you all a good diet and hopefully, that should help."

I'm overly optimistic. She's so frail—but I've seen miracles happen before and I'm not willing to give up on her yet. We need to get her back. Keep her safe.

She puts the bark in her mouth and chews before closing her eyes and sighing.

Mason looks up at Cheng. "We should move her as soon as possible. Get her settled in the boat while we still have time. I'd hate to have to rush down the stairs or into the boat with her."

Cheng nods. "Yes. We will take her while the others get our things organised." He looks at me. "If you would assist us once again, I would be grateful. My mother has a bag in her cupboard. If you could pack some clothes for her?"

I stand. "Of course. I'd be happy to."

I rise from the edge of the bed and get the bag, filling it with clothes and shoes, while Cheng gently picks his mother up from the bed and Mason follows him out of the room. I look around me, trying to decide what else to put in—personal things she might want. I wish I'd been able to do that myself, but I was up in the mountains when the water rose, so quickly most people didn't have time to get to safety, let alone collect their stuff. And for those who did go back, they didn't stand a chance. Even a lot of the people trying to get to the safety of the mountains didn't make it, swept away by the water while still in their cars, the traffic jams stopping people moving. That's what happened to my parents and sister. I was on the phone to them when the water took them, heard the horror in their voices, the panic . . .

In that one moment, I'd lost everything except Mason and what we had in our hiking packs.

Apart from my family, photos are the things I miss the most—my memories feel tenuous without something to tether them in the here and now. And I hate that my mum and dad's faces, my younger sister's, grow less vivid with each passing day.

I grab some photos off the nightstand and her brush, some jewellery that looks sentimental. I hope it's enough to make her feel at home, back in the Territories.

I carry the bag and my medic kit back out to the living area. Ming is waiting there with the children, the oldest one with a backpack on his shoulders, just as Cheng and Mason come back up. Mason's face is pale and I can see his pain in the way he moves.

"Are you okay?" I ask quietly, not wanting to draw attention to him.

"Yeah. Bit sore but I'll be okay. I think we need to get going though."

I turn to the family. "Are you ready to go?"

"Yes." Cheng looks around the penthouse. "Yu

is already down in the boat with her Grandmother. I am waiting for An to get our weapons, our jewellery."

I share a glance with Mason and he looks as surprised as me.

"Cheng, we don't have time. They'll be coming. It doesn't matter. Leave all that stuff here. We need to make you safe."

"No, no. We must take some. How else will we bargain for what we need? How will I make sure my family is provided for?"

Mason gives a low growl and I can feel his frustration, layered with his pain and anxiety. "One bag," he says at last. "You can pack one bag and we'll lock the rest away. Come back for it another time."

"No, we must take more."

"No." Mason sags a little and I wrap my arm around him, supporting some of his weight. God, we need to get away! Can't they understand that? I don't know what Cheng sees in my face but he moves forward as if to help, before stopping and nodding his head.

"One bag. That will be enough."

I help Mason sit on the couch and soon Cheng returns with a bag in his hand, stuffed so full the zipper won't shut properly. Mason goes to grab one of the family's other bags but I stop him, picking it up myself.

"Not a chance," I say, frowning at him. "At this

rate, you're barely going to make it down the stairs."

He kisses the top of my head and we move through the lounge room, following the others out of the door and down the stairs. Cheng has one of the kids in his arms and I can see how worried he is, the way he keeps looking back at Ming, his whole body tense. I can only imagine the emotions running through him— anxiety about whether he's making the right decision for his family, fear over the threats already hanging over their heads and what they might face in the Territories.

I can hardly believe the bravery it must take to do this—to go with practical strangers to a place where you don't know if you'll be accepted or not. Where some of the people you're hoping to live with are thinking of hurting you just because they can. And taking this risk, not only for you, but for your family as well. A surge of protectiveness rears up in me as I watch the older child make his way down the stairs, dwarfed by the backpack, and I know I'm going to do everything I can to make sure they're safe.

An climbs into the dinghy, holding it steady while Cheng helps Ming and the children in. He turns and offers his hand to me. It's been a long time since I needed help to get in a boat but I don't want to offend him so I take it, smiling at him. I don't feel so bad when he helps Mason in as well.

THE RISE

Mason's skin is even paler and there's a greyish tinge to it. My heart lurches as I watch him settle himself on the seat, his shirt drenched in sweat, his breathing shallow. I take his hand, anxiety gripping my body, as if every single one of my organs is squeezing, twisting. Shit. We need to get back. Get back and give him time to really heal.

Fucking Authority. Fucking Carl. I don't think I've ever hated anyone as much as I hate him in this moment.

We're all loaded into the dinghy and Mason's boat is in sight when we hear it. Another boat engine. Coming closer.

I pull on the oars so hard it's a wonder I don't put my shoulders out. God, oh God. Is it them? Coming already? And what will they do? If they were willing to stab Mason—leave him for dead—what will they do to all of us? I know Alex hunts with a bow and arrow . . . and I know he's a good shot. Is he a killer though? If it actually came to that, could he kill people he knew? After all, it'd only been Carl who'd actually hurt Mason . . .

I never thought I'd be having these thoughts about people I've lived with peacefully for the last three years; people I've helped when they were hurt. People I thought were my community. My new family.

It's as if we're all on super-speed as we row over

to Mason's boat and start unloading everyone. Or maybe that's what the adrenalin is making me believe. And yet, it still doesn't feel fast enough. Nowhere close.

Hurry. Hurry, hurry, hurry.

It's the only word my brain seems to connect with.

The two younger kids, as well as Ming and Mason, are on board by the time the boat comes into sight. I recognise it instantly as Rosa's boat from Territory Two. Carl and Alex are up the front and I can see their eyes widen as they catch sight of us—see Mason's boat and realise he's still alive; see me, urging the others up, tying the dinghy with hands so unsteady I wonder if it'd be better just to leave it.

And then I'm up on deck, Cheng and An following on my heels, and Mason is starting the engines. Damn saving petrol. We need to get away.

"Kate. Mason. Don't be stupid," Alex calls out to us as we start skirt around a building. "We're not going to hurt anyone."

There's no way I believe that. Not even a small part of my brain thinks there's a chance that might be true. If they weren't going to hurt anyone, they wouldn't be here. Especially Carl, who still hasn't spoken. Instead, he's staring at Mason as if he's seen a ghost.

And then, so quickly it catches me by surprise,

anger crosses Carl's face, distorting it to the point where I wonder if I've ever really known him—this person who fought for us, for our lives, for our place in the new world. How can this be the man who thanked me when I stitched up his leg up from a nasty gash a year ago? The man who bought two eggs over for Ellie on her last birthday, so she could have a special sweet sixteen breakfast? I don't know who this man is but he's definitely not the Carl I thought I knew.

"Kate!" he yells at me. "Don't do this. Mason's been outlawed from the Territories. He can't go back. If you go with them, you'll be outlawed too. You'll lose your home."

"How is *he* outlawed when you're the one who tried to kill him?" I scream back, even though I know it's not going to do any good. He'll never admit to what he did, otherwise why would he be here? Why would they all be here?

"I don't know what he's told you but he was the one who attacked me first. It was self-defence."

I can't believe that's the story he's going with, although that's probably naïve of me. If you're willing to kill someone, then lying's only a minor offence in comparison—I guess I thought he would've come up with something better.

I stick my middle finger up at him, beyond words,

and sick of being scared, of giving in to the fear and flashbacks, of living in the past. I need to do what's right now. Next to me, Mason chuckles softly and pulls me closer to him. Our boat moves between two buildings and then we open the throttle, heading out towards the open sea.

Then, to my horror, I realise the others aren't stopping. They're following us! Coming after us! Shit. That wasn't the plan. They were supposed to stop and go into the unit, looking for the weapons, the jewellery— giving us time to get away and make sure the family were safe! They were supposed to have stopped!

"We don't have it!" I call out, panic clear in my voice.

Because we don't have any way to defend ourselves, unless Cheng and An have packed something in the bag we can use. But the kids? Their Grandmother? How can we protect everyone, especially with Mason still recovering?

I move to the back of the boat, leaning on the rails, and gesture for Mason to reduce the throttle. The motor reduces to a low hum. Thankfully Carl does the same.

"We don't have the weapons or the jewellery," I call out to them. "You can have it all!"

"No!" Cheng yells at me, but I don't care. Not

one little bit. It's just stuff. Objects. And I'm not willing to risk Mason's life for objects.

"Just let us take the family down the coast, make them safe. We won't go to the Territories, and we won't come back here. But we don't have the weapons! They're back there. In the unit still."

It has the desired effect. I can see them talking to each other, arguing, and then Carl waves his hand to whoever's driving the boat and they turn, heading back towards the city. We're safe.

For the moment.

CHAPTER SIX

We sail through the day and night, the direction of the wind meaning it takes longer to get back than it did going down—even though we use the motor now and again. The sun is only just rising at the end of the second night when we get to the Territories. I can't believe it's only been a few days since my whole life turned upside down. Again.

This is worse, in some ways, than the Rise. This is a betrayal. A betrayal that jeopardises the peace we've all worked so hard for. And now, I'm angry. Angry they've made this decision for us. Angry that their greed has threatened the people who are important to me.

Fuck them!

There's no point in hiding anymore. They know Mason's alive. They know what we've done. But they seemed to believe the lie about us taking the family down the coast. Maybe they don't think we'd be stupid enough to try to go against them, to try to make the people of the Territories go against Carl . . . That arrogance might just play to our advantage.

We have a loose plan. As soon as we get back, we need to talk to Gavin and work out if he's on the same side as Carl and the rest of the Authority. He hadn't been at the meeting to agree, or disagree, so it's hard to know where he stands. It's a risk but it feels like it's our only option.

Other than leaving the Territory.

And I can't do that to Ellie. I won't abandon her, and I'd never ask her to leave another place she calls home.

When we moor Mason's boat beside my own, Ellie comes out on deck, a relieved smile on her face. I hug her as we come onto the boat and she hugs me back, holding tight like she was worried she was never going to get a chance to do it again.

"They left in the boat," she murmurs into my shoulder. "Rosa, Alex, Zack. And Carl." I hear the hurt clearly in her voice. "I tried to delay them, stop them, but I couldn't."

I squeeze her tighter. "It's okay. We're okay. And we got the family out. The older kids and Mason will be staying with us tonight, while everyone else stays on Mason's boat."

She nods and then finally lets me go, only to hug Mason. She's a lot more gentle with him though. I help An and Yu on board and introduce them to Ellie. They give her shy smiles. It's weird to think this is the first time they've met someone close to their age in the last five years. Ellie takes them into the cabin to show them where they'll be staying.

I turn to Mason, touching his face with my fingertips. "How are you?"

He gives me a half-smile and laughs. "Sore. Tired. All the things you'd probably expect for someone who's been stabbed, nearly drowned, kissed a beautiful woman and then gone on a rescue attempt. God, I'm in a frigging twisted fairy tale."

"Come on then, Prince Charming." I take his hand and lead him inside my cabin. "I need to check that wound."

He grins, a true one this time. "You just want to get my clothes off."

I smile back at him, even though I can feel the heat on my face. "You wish."

He chuckles as I shut the door, taking his shirt

off and standing beside the bed. His skin is tanned and muscular from all the time he's spent in the sun and working on the boat, and it's tempting to run my fingers down his chest now I'm allowed to.

Later though. Once all of this has been sorted out—one way or another.

The bandage is starting to look dirty, stained with sweat, and I take it off him, looking at where I'd stitched his skin up. I'm relieved to see the wound's still looking okay—no sign of infection—and I wash it gently before grabbing some more turmeric powder to sprinkle over it, smoothing it over his skin. He leans down and kisses me, softly, like a relieved sigh at the end of a long day. I wish it was. But our day's only beginning and I don't think it's going to get easier.

I wrap a clean bandage around his torso and we head back to the main cabin. Ellie is waiting for us, impatient, as if she half expected us to sneak off without her. Which would probably be for the best but I couldn't do that to her. She's right. She's not a kid anymore and she's got a right to say what happens in her community.

"An and Lu are having a lie down," she says. "What's the plan now?"

"Cheng's with the rest of the family on Mason's boat. He only agreed to stay there when we said we'd bring Gavin back to meet with him."

He wasn't happy but it was the only way to get him to stay with his family where we could keep them all relatively safe.

"We'd better go and see Gavin then." Ellie narrows her eyes at me, as if she's waiting for me to argue with her. I know there's no point though.

Climbing into the dinghy with Ellie and Mason, we make our way over to land, the sun well and truly up now. Others are making their way over too, and they're all happy to see Mason, asking what he's found on this journey. No-one seems concerned about his well-being, and a bubble of hope rises up in my chest as we get out of the dinghy, making me a little breathless. If no one knows about Mason's injury then it means no-one from our Territory was in on it. . . hopefully.

And then I see Gavin. His eyes widen as he notices Mason and my heart sinks. He knows, then. He was part of it.

I grab Mason's hand, wanting to pull him back, pull him away. Protect him, somehow. Surely Gavin won't try anything in daylight, out here in public, not with so many people around. Ellie looks nervous too, and she takes a half-step back towards the dinghy.

Gavin stands in front of us, his eyes skimming over Mason's face, his body, like he's trying to understand something.

"You decided to come back," he says at last.

Mason narrows his eyes. "Yeah, back from the dead."

"What?" says Gavin, looking genuinely confused.

I feel a twinge of hope. "Where do you think Mason's come back from?"

Gavin gestures in the general direction of Authority house. "Carl said you'd left after the meeting the other night. I couldn't get to it—my boat was leaking and I had to repair it. He said you called the meeting so you could ask to be released from the Territories."

Mason's hands go to his hips. "Why the hell would you believe that? Why would I want to be released from the Territories?"

I might be imagining it, but Gavin's cheeks go slightly red and he doesn't meet my eyes. "Didn't sound like something you'd do, to be honest. But he said you and Kate had a . . . falling out."

I frown at him. "A falling out?"

"Yeah. He said you'd . . . well, that you'd propositioned Mason and he wanted to leave." Gavin seems to find something very interesting to look at on the ground. "That's why I wasn't sure what to say when you asked if he was back."

Mason lets out a sharp laugh but pulls it in quickly when I glare at him. "Nothing like that happened, Gav.

And I would've come and told you if I was ever going to leave." Mason takes my hand and Gavin gives a quick nod in acknowledgement.

"What really happened at the meeting, then?"

Blunt, straight to the point—and right at this moment, I'm glad he isn't someone who dances around the hard questions. We don't have time for that.

Mason tells him what's happened. Everything. The argument, the stabbing, the journey to rescue the family . . . even the fact Carl and the others followed us there. Gavin's lips get thinner and thinner as the story unfolds. But he doesn't interrupt. He just listens. At the end, he lets out a gust of breath.

"Jesus. It's hard for me to get my head around, to be honest."

I nod. "I can understand that. It was hard for me too."

He narrows his eyes at me. "You should've told me when you found Mason. I knew something was going on. You seemed really worried—tense. And Alex was . . . well, more Alex than he normally is. I couldn't work out what was happening."

I nod, feeling guilt swirl in my stomach. "I know. I'm sorry. I just didn't know who I could trust. Mason told me not to tell the Authority before he blacked out. I wasn't sure who was included in that."

"I can respect that," he says, hands moving to his hips. "So, what are we doing now? I'm assuming you have the family here with you?"

"Yeah," Mason says. "They're here. Split between my boat and Kate's. The Grandmother isn't well. She needs help. Medical care. Good food."

"We have to let them stay," Ellie says, stepping forward, hands on her hips, mirroring Gavin, like she's ready to argue with anyone who thinks differently. "It's only fair. If someone wants to stay—wants to be a part of our Territory—then we should give them the opportunity."

Gavin nods. "I agree. I think we can offer them a home, if they want one. But we need to put this to a vote, the same as in the old days. This one obviously can't be settled by the Authority alone, and given what's happened, we don't know what the repercussions are going to be. Our community has the right to know what they're getting in to—what they're agreeing to. If we let this family in, then we are basically staging a mutiny. And if the other territories turn against us, then it's going to make our lives a lot more difficult. After a few years of peace, not everyone's going to be okay with that, just to save one family."

He's right. Even though I just want a decision to be made—want the family settled—our people need to understand what that might mean for them.

Gavin turns, letting out a loud whistle that carries up over the terraces.

"Everybody in the shed," he calls out loudly. "We're having a Territory One meeting."

I give Mason a wry smile. No, Gavin definitely isn't one to muck around. Everyone listens, even if they do shoot us confused looks as we walk up to the shed with Gavin. It only takes a few minutes before everyone's settled, some sitting, some leaning against the walls. Ellie perches near the door, looking down to the boats.

"What's this about, Gavin?" Trish calls out.

Gavin holds up his hand, acknowledging the question. "I've got some information I think you all need to be aware of. And then I want to have a community vote."

The hushed talk swells in the enclosed space and Gavin holds his hand up again until everyone's quiet. He looks at Mason. "I want you to take off your shirt," he says, and even though Mason raises his eyebrows, he does what Gavin asks.

There are a few wolf whistles from the community and I grin at the blush on Mason's cheeks, but I can see what Gavin's doing. It's a good plan.

Gavin points to the bandage. "Mason was stabbed a few days ago."

THE RISE

A loud buzz fills the room almost instantly, people cursing and yelling out questions.

George moves forward and clears his throat, his voice only just able to be heard over the noise. "Who did it?"

Standing up straighter, Gavin looks around at everyone so that they quieten down before he answers. "Carl."

The noise grows even louder and I can see the confusion and anger on people's faces. Gavin whistles again, the noise shrill in the confined space. But it's effective at shutting everyone up.

"Right. I need you all to listen. No more interruptions until I've explained everything."

He waits a moment and everyone is quiet, waiting. And then he tells them everything, as only Gavin can. No excess words, no softness—blunt and to the point.

"So," he finishes. "That's it. That's what happened. And now we have a family out there, waiting to be made welcome. That's what I want you all to vote on. Are you happy to let this family into our Territory? Raise your hand if you're happy to include them in our bigger family, even though it might cause more problems."

But before anyone can do that, Ellie yells from

the door at the back of the shed, her face red. "They're out there! Carl and Alex. And they're about to get onto Mason's boat!"

CHAPTER SEVEN

Mason and I push through the crowd and out the door of the shed. I don't know how he keeps up with me, but he does, and we make it down to the water's edge before anyone else, leaping into the dinghy. I steady the oars as Mason unties the rope and, as we're about to pull away, Gavin and Ellie grab the edge and pull themselves in. Around us, Territory One residents are getting into their own dinghies. I'm grateful for the back-up, grateful they care enough—even if it's only because they care about us, not yet knowing the Li family. Or maybe they just care enough about living in a world where people look after each other, making sure we create the world we want our children to live in.

I can hear the yelling on Mason's boat when we're halfway there. My heart's firmly lodged in my throat, making it hard to breathe.

Shit. Shit, shit, shit!

If Alex and Carl hurt anybody, I'm going to kill the two of them myself. Horribly. Make them suffer. I pull harder on the oars, puffing with each stroke. Ellie's on her knees on the front seat, leaning forward as if it's going to make us go faster and Mason's face is hard. Fierce.

"Carl!" Gavin roars and, on Mason's boat, there's silence for a moment. A silence that feels even worse than the yelling. But then Carl is out on the deck, a knife clutched in his hand. My heart freezes. There's no blood on it though—none I can see anyway. I feel nauseous at the thought of what he might've done—at what I know he's capable of—and swallow hard, fighting it back.

"Gavin," Carl calls back. "This is none of your business. This is Authority business. These people are here illegally."

"Last time I checked, I *was* part of the Authority. And I didn't realise you had to be legal to be made welcome here. Whatever the hell that means."

Even from there, I can see the anger on Carl's face. "Leave it, Gavin. I started the Territories—and the Authority. I get to make the decision on this. And this is none of your fucking business!"

We're close enough to the boat now that we could climb aboard . . . if Carl wasn't standing there with a knife. I can see Alex on the other side of the boat, keeping the people from our Territory away.

"When you stab someone from my Territory, it becomes my business."

"It was self-defence!" says Carl. "He was trying to kill me! And now he's brought these people here when I told him not to. He lied to me. To us. He doesn't *care* about the safety of our community."

"And that's why *you're* the one standing there with a fucking knife in your hand!" Gavin yells at him. "Jesus Christ, Carl, what are you doing? These people aren't going to hurt anyone. They just want somewhere to live."

"We can't have any more people here. We've got enough and any more will mean we don't have enough for us. They can go and find somewhere else. I don't want to hurt them but they don't belong here."

"Yeah right," I yell back. "You were willing to kill them for their belongings."

"That's not true," says Carl. He turns his body slightly, gesturing towards our community members on their boats. "I'm not here to steal anything, or hurt anyone, or whatever Mason and Katie have been telling you. I started the Territories. I brought you all together—

I'm always looking out for your best interests. Just head on back to your jobs and we can settle this civilly."

Nobody leaves.

"Where are Cheng and Ming and the children?" I yell at him, just wanting to jump into the water and climb on the boat—move, do something, anything! If he's hurt them . . .

He sneers at me. "They're in the cabin. They should never have been allowed to come here. But you and Mason had to interfere. You couldn't just leave it be."

"You told Mason to kill them!" I scream at him.

"That's not true."

"Carl, please, don't. Let them go." The hurt is clear in Ellie's voice—the plea to this person she's look up to—respected and loved—that he'll listen . . . that he'll change back to who she thought he was.

"Ellie. You need to leave. You don't know what's going on here. These people are dangerous. We can't let them into our lives. I'm doing it to protect everyone."

She shakes her head, the disappointment easy to see on her face, before she sits up straight, her eyes narrowed. "They're not dangerous. I've met them. They're nice people. They just want a place to live. And all you want is their weapons and gold and jewellery." She looks back at Mason. "And you stabbed Mason. Tried to kill him. One of our own. My friend. It's you who doesn't deserve to be a part of this community."

"You don't know what happened, Ellie. You're too young to understand."

"Fuck off!" The words ring out over the water and there's a second of silence before a few people cheer. The sound seems to bring a subtle shift in power.

Carl looks around him, like he can't believe what's happening.

George—sweet, gentle George—calls out from the other side of Mason's boat. "Well, if you've got nothing to hide—if everything's above board like you say—you won't mind if we go and have a look at what you've got on Rosa's boat."

Carl hurries around the other side to stand next to Alex.

"Stay away from the boat," he says, as if he still thinks he's in charge. Delusional. Or maybe he's trying to bluff. "There's nothing in there that's of concern to anyone else."

But it's too late. There are already three boat loads of people rowing over there and Carl can only watch, his face going red.

I take advantage of the distraction and grab the rope hanging off the rail, hauling myself up on deck. Gavin's quick to follow me up and Carl whirls, snarling as he sees us. Snarling! Like a rabid animal. Jesus!

"You've wrecked everything!" he yells at me, charging at us. The look on his face is so angry—so animalistic—I can't stop myself from stepping back, tripping over a length of rope rolled on the deck.

He pounces on me, grabbing my arm and hauling me up, the knife pressed into my side. I freeze. As does everyone else. My eyes flick to Mason, still in the dinghy—he's watching us, eyes wide, hands clenched into fists.

Gavin holds his hands up slowly. "Carl, you don't want to do this. Not to Kate. She's never done anything but good in our community."

Carl pushes the knife harder into my side and I gasp, the pain taking me by surprise. He hasn't pushed it in far but I can feel a trickle of blood run down my side. The bastard's cut me! Anger wells up, filling me with a rage I haven't felt before.

Mason stands up in the dinghy. "Let her go, you fucking arsehole!"

"Shut up. Just shut up!" Carl screams and I realise he's beyond rational thought. We aren't going to be able to talk him out of this. And I'm certainly not ready to die under his knife. I survived the Rise, for God's sake! This can't be how it ends.

There's a shout from Rosa's boat and we look

over. Rosa and Zack are being held by two of the residents and George has an armload of guns he's holding up. Proof of everything we've told the residents.

"No!" Carl says, looking around at the people watching him from the boats surrounding us. "You don't understand. It was for all of you. To make our community stronger. Weapons to protect us and gold and stones to be able to trade. Everything I did . . . everything . . . was to make us stronger!"

"And what about the family?" Gavin asks, his voice low.

Carl snorts. "What about them? They aren't part of our community. They don't deserve to be here. We've built this up. All of us. Five years. *I* brought us all together. *I* made it so we aren't fighting anymore. *I* get to say who comes here!"

"No," Gavin says. "You don't. Not anymore."

Carl lunges at him, the knife cutting me deeper as he does. He knocks Gavin over, pushing him onto the deck, the knife at his throat. I can hear Carl panting, can see the sweat on his forehead.

"Carl, please. Don't." One hand is pressing my side, trying to stop the bleeding but I have the other hand out in front of me, begging him. "Please."

Gavin is watching him, eyes not leaving Carl's face. "Carl, get a grip. You don't have to do this."

And then everything seems to happen in slow motion. I see Cheng's son come up on the deck, his face serious, watching us as Carl brings the knife up, away from Gavin, his eyes on the young boy. As Carl goes to lunge at him, I move too, grabbing the half crowbar that's attached to the outside of the cabin.

And I swing it.

The sound of the bar hitting Carl's skull is a sound unlike anything I've heard before. And one I never want to hear again.

I drop the bar, standing in shock at what I've done, unable to see anything except Carl's crushed skull.

His staring eyes.

The blood.

And then Mason's arms are around me, turning me towards him, and I don't have to see it anymore.

EPILOGUE

It took a long time for the community to get back to normal.

The fall out from Carl's death—from our Authority taking their power too far—created ripples big enough to swamp us all. Even though the majority of people didn't agree with Carl's ideas, there were still enough who believed in blindly following the Authority to create discord amongst the Territories. There was even talk of Mason being put on trial to find out the "real" reason Carl stabbed him—if it had been self-defence, as Carl had said. Thankfully, that idea was quickly squashed by Gavin, and nobody was willing to push back too hard.

I was cleared of any wrongdoing without the need for a trial. There'd been more than enough people to attest to Carl's anger and the fact he'd tried to kill Gavin and Cheng's son. I was glad. It's hard enough as it is to deal with the flashbacks that still plague me. I'm starting to feel stronger though. More alive. More . . . me. Maybe not the Kate I was before the Rise but a Kate that has part of that girl in her still.

Mason's helped with that too. It's amazing how the threat of almost losing more people we love has moved our relationship along, and I can't stop rubbing my swelling stomach, impatient to meet our new little one when he or she decides to come.

The Li family were settled into our community fairly quickly and while, for the main part, this has been good for everyone, it's taken some patience—both for people to accept someone new, and for the whole family who haven't had to deal with other people or other rules for five years. But the humanity evident in the Territory's protection of them has continued and the pieces of our community are fitting together.

It took a long time to sort out the Authority and to decide if we still wanted it in our life—not just for Territory One, but for all the Territories. We were all affected by the injustice of the situation, and thankfully, what could have resulted in one territory against eight, ended with us all pretty much on the same side. Six and Seven were the first to side with us—Chris and Lisa pleased to be able to stand up for their beliefs rather than being overruled by Carl and the rest of the Authority— and then the rest followed. We still have borders to our communities, but they've become a lot more fluid and welcoming over time. In the end, it was decided Alex, Rosa and Zack wouldn't be banished from our community—although there were people crying out for their blood. I wouldn't have minded seeing Alex and Rosa leave, but the truth was that they hadn't actually physically hurt anyone—they'd been stupid enough to be sucked into Carl's plans but who knew what bullshit he'd fed them. Besides, I wouldn't wish the life they would be forced to live outside the Territories on anyone, and they all had families who'd be devastated to lose them.

They'd all been stripped of their representative responsibilities, and accepted the condition that they'd never take them up again. In the end, new representatives were picked—but voted on by each Territory this time, rather than chosen solely by Carl. And after lots of arguments and discussions, it was decided we no longer needed an overall leader . . . Carl's betrayal too fresh in our minds to try that again.

But I'm still proud of what we've managed to pull together since the Rise. The humanity we've built into our lives, the fact that we aren't just a bunch of terrified people, struggling to make sense of our new world, but can instead, still be caring and accepting. Still be able to think about a life we'd all love to build rather than just surviving.

I don't know what the world will be like as my little one grows. But I'm hopeful. And maybe that's all that matters.

ABOUT THE AUTHOR

A writer of copious amounts of words – just because if they didn't come out, she's sure they'd make her head explode – Sue-Ellen is an international author with four published stories: Aquila, When Henry Met Gina, The Jade Goddess and Streamer, with her children's picture book, The Jacket, released in May, 2019. From being an avid reader and writer as a child to studying literature at university, she's always loved the written word and where it can transport her.

In her 'other' life, Sue-Ellen is a social worker and lives in Central Queensland with her ever-patient family and a menagerie of animals, including snakes, turtles, lizards, dogs and fish. She's an eternal optimist who enjoys making things difficult for her protagonists but loves a satisfying ending.

http://www.sueellenpashley.com/

ABOUT DEADSET PRESS

Deadset Press is the publishing imprint for Aussie
Speculative Fiction – a community aimed at supporting
Australian and Kiwi authors. You can learn more at:

www.aussiespeculativefiction.com

ABOUT THE SERIES

Drowned Earth is a series of eight standalone novellas, set in a shared world.

Prequel: Shards of Silver by Alanah Andrews
Debbie is on board a ship when an asteroid collides with Antarctica, causing a tsunami. And it's heading her way…
(eBook Only: Free Download)

Submerged City by Austin P. Sheehan
Melbourne is under martial law, overseen by general Messinger—an extremist who believes the flood is God's retribution against the left-wing agenda...

The Rise by Sue-Ellen Pashley
The great Rise means that resources are scarce and not readily shared. But with her best friend's life at stake, along with some stranded refugees, Katie James knows she must prove there's more to being human than just existing. Even if that puts her on the same kill list.

Fire Over Troubled Water by Nick Marone
Despite winds, torrential rains, storms, and bushfires, a fresh water merchant searches for his lost daughter among the autonomous island communities of flooded eastern New South Wales.

Tides of War by Marcus Turner

After discovering a strange man in a row boat, Maria wages war on the lotus cities—clandestine floating communities off the coast of Victoria that are reserved for the wealthy.

The Jindabyne Secret by Jo Hart

With nothing but a map and a rickety solar truck, Jax journeys to the top secret fresh water facility at Lake Jindabyne—one of the few fresh water lakes left in Australia. What he discovers there could be the key to saving his whole community, as long as the government doesn't kill him first.

River of Diamonds by S. M. Isaac

Who would want to leave one of the last idyllic settlements since the Rise? Rosa has a map, a mercenary, and a hope to salvage a future for the world.

Salvaged by C.A. Clark

Cassie lives in the safe haven of academics on the anchored city of new Melbourne. After a diving incident she is rescued by a territorial beach combing gang who trade goods washed up by the frequent storms. Cassie wishes she had never taken her home for granted.

Emoto's Promise by Shel Calopa

Five hundred years after the flood, can Macie defeat the technology which has enslaved the last remaining humans in the walled city of Darwin?

ALSO BY DEADSET PRESS

Annual Anthologies

Beginnings: Australian Speculative Fiction Vol. 1

Journeys: Australian Speculative Fiction Vol. 2

Zodiac Series

Capricorn

Aquarius

Pisces

www.aussiespeculativefiction.com

www.ingramcontent.com/pod-product-compliance
Lightning Source LLC
Chambersburg PA
CBHW020231120726
47903CB00008B/2636